DEBORAH
BEDFORD
and her novels

"Deborah Bedford grabs the reader
by the heart and doesn't let go."
—#1 *New York Times* bestselling author
Debbie Macomber

"Deborah Bedford...will inspire readers
with [a] message of hope and healing through
the power of love."
—CBA *Marketplace* on *Blessing*

"From beginning to end Bedford...
calls upon every emotion imaginable."
—*Christian Reading* on *Blessing*

"Both heartwarming and melancholy,
Bedford's...poignant tale will find a home
in all collections."
—*Library Journal* on *A Rose by the Door*

"[A] well-told tale that should appeal to readers of
faith who enjoy an inspirational love story wrapped
around deeper issues."
—*Publishers Weekly* on *When You Believe*

Dear Reader,

I was inspired to write *Family Matters* years ago by the doctor who delivered my daughter Avery. At the same time he was helping us bring a new life into the world, his own mother was seriously ill and he could do nothing to help her. I was struck by the irony of his life—being in a position to heal strangers but unable to help someone he loved dearly. For this story, I decided if the hero couldn't help his son, I'd have him trust that God could heal his broken marriage instead.

After writing seven romance novels, I began to feel the Holy Spirit nudging me, calling me to let go of my writing career, to turn it over to Him. For three years I wasn't able to publish anything. Then, in a series of events that could only be the Lord's work (which proves God has a wonderful sense of humor), I began my career in Christian publishing.

As well as having the opportunity to cowrite with speaker and personality Joyce Meyer (we're working on our second book now, and our first, *The Penny*, is soon to be a motion picture), I've had the opportunity to revise some older stories so they can now be republished for God's glory. *Family Matters* is just such a book. It was originally published under the title *After the Promise*. I hope you enjoy this revised version, that you find some new surprises, that you forgive the rough spots and that you walk away inspired to lay your life where the adventure truly starts...in God's hands!

In His glorious love,

P.S. I'd love to hear from you and to pray for you. E-mail me by visiting my Web site at www.deborahbedfordbooks.com or write me via snail mail at: P.O. 9175, Jackson, WY 83001

DEBORAH BEDFORD

Family Matters

Refreshed version of *After the Promise*
newly revised by author.

Steeple
Hill®

Published by Steeple Hill Books™

STEEPLE HILL BOOKS

Steeple
Hill®

ISBN-13: 978-0-373-78613-8
ISBN-10: 0-373-78613-1

FAMILY MATTERS

This is the revised text of the work, which was first published by Harlequin Enterprises Limited in 1993.

Copyright © 1993 by Deborah Pigg Bedford

Revised text copyright © 2008 by Deborah Pigg Bedford

www.SteepleHill.com

Printed in U.S.A.

Long ago,
 real life
  brought
   fairy tales
    and castles.
Sitting on the edge of my
    bed
    I'd bounce
    and be a princess on a
    pony.
Now
 I know it's the daily things,
  the love
   life
     brings,
  football by the fire,
  cookie dough in a bowl,
  our son running home from
    school,
    his hair like the
    yellow meadow
    in September.
Now
 our daughter bounces on the bed.
 We watch her playing
   princess on a pony.
Someday, too,
  she will see
   the fairy tale's in
    you
     and me,
     a reflection of
       strict reality,
     and our
      own
       blessed
        measure
         of
          victory.
                    —dpb

As always, to Jack. I love you.

To those who need to let go, who need to take God's healing and His gentle victory.

Chapter One

"**D**r. Stratton." The desk clerk flagged Michael down as he strode past the nurses' station. "Your sitter phoned. She said she couldn't get you on your cell. She needs you to call home right away."

Michael reached for the phone she set on the counter for him and punched in his number. When the babysitter answered, he wasted no time greeting her. "What's wrong, Heather?"

"Cody has a fever of 104 degrees. I think he's really sick. What should I do?"

Michael frowned. Cody hadn't even had a cold for months. He must have been exposed to something at school. But what kind of flu bug would cause a fever that high? He'd have to phone Jennie and find out if his friends had been sick. "Just keep him comfortable until I get home. There's a bottle of children's acetaminophen in the medicine cabinet. Give him four of those. If his fever doesn't start dropping after that, call me back." He handed the phone to the clerk.

"Dr. Stratton. Your patient in 208 is totally dilated," an O.B. nurse informed him as she passed. "The baby's head is at plus one."

"Tell them I'm on my way." He washed up quickly and donned his scrubs. When he hurried into room 208, Julie Miller was just beginning to push. She strained, her hair plastered against her forehead with sweat. At last she fell back against the pillow. "I can't do this!" she told anyone who would listen. "I never intended to do this without *drugs,*" she said, half teasing, and completely serious. "*Drugs,* Dr. Stratton. Anesthesia. Pain relief."

"The baby's coming too fast, Julie. What you've got here is a nice natural childbirth. Something a lot of people are going to envy you for."

"But I…can't…"

"Oh, yes. You *can.*" He moved to the foot of the birthing bed, pulled up the stool and sat down. "Let's have a baby here. I can see the head."

"Can you?" she asked breathlessly, raising her head slightly as tears of exertion streamed down her cheeks.

"It's right here. I see dark hair, lots of it. Another few pushes and this will be over. Come on, Julie."

Michael had seen hundreds of women through labor and delivery. But he still couldn't do it without feeling a little twinge of pride and sadness, thinking of his own son's birth eight years ago. Jennie had been so brave. And Cody had been such a gift to both of them. There had been a time when they both thought that loving their son might be enough to save their marriage. But it hadn't happened that way.

"I feel the contraction coming. It's coming. I don't… "

"You can do it, Julie," her husband said, encouraging her.

"Focus all your energy on this push," Michael urged. "Let your body do this for you. Keep your knees wide. Hold on. Hold on."

"Good," his nurse joined in, cheering her on. "Perfect."

In spite of the fast, easy birth, this patient would need an episiotomy. He performed it quickly as Julie Miller began to strain again.

The baby's head emerged. A shoulder came next and then the rest of the newborn slipped out, a fine, healthy boy, already bleating for his mother. Michael handed her the baby as the nurse wrapped Julie in warm blankets. "Thanks," she whispered.

After Michael showed the father how to cut the cord and allowed the proud new parents to count fingers and toes, he examined the infant himself and gave him a high Apgar score. "Congratulations!" He shook the father's hand before he tucked his charts beneath his arm. Then he touched Julie's arm. "Good work, Mom."

With that, he swung briskly out of room 208 and headed for the fourth floor and his next patient. He looked forward to his visits with Bill Josephs. "Well, Bill," he said, leaning back against the wall and studying his elderly client from a distance. "You look good enough to run a marathon."

"I am *looking* good," the old man bellowed at him. "I am *feeling* good. When're you gonna send me home, Doc?"

"Well—" Michael appeared to consider as he winked at Bill's wife, adjusting his bedside manner to fit comfortable country folks and friends "—how about tomorrow?"

"Yes!" Bill lifted a fist in victory. "Dr. Michael, it's about time you let me out of this confounded place."

"You don't follow my orders, you'll be right back here." Michael scribbled a prescription and handed the little paper to Bill's wife, Marge. "You take that three times a day and you'll be good as new."

"What is this stuff?" Bill chortled. "Viagra?"

Michael had known the Josephs since he'd graduated from med school. Bill's jokes didn't faze him at all anymore. "You rest every afternoon. The minute the farm news report is over and you've eaten lunch, I want you flat on your back for thirty minutes."

"I'll make him do it," Marge promised.

"No smoking. And when you're drinking coffee with your buddies down at the Ferris Dairy Queen, make sure it's decaf."

"You gonna make me drink unleaded for the rest of my life?" Bill asked.

"Yeah." Michael slapped the man's chart shut. "I am. I'll see you in my office in two weeks."

"We'll be there," Marge promised again. "I know how to boss this old coot around."

Michael hugged her. He didn't hug many of his patients, but the Josephs were practically family. "Take good care of him. You're going to have him around for a long time."

Marge shook her head and grinned. "That's what I was afraid of."

Michael hurried upstairs to sign Bill's release papers. As he scrawled his signature, his BlackBerry sprang to life. When he went to answer it, he lost the call. Michael shook his head. The concrete walls of the hospital wreaked havoc on his cell-phone signal. He checked the screen to see if it had been his office trying to reach him. But it wasn't. His home number had been calling. Cody's babysitter again.

The hospital pager on his belt went off. He headed to the nearest house phone and picked it up. "Heather Rogers is on the line," the operator told him. "She says it's an emergency."

"Put her through," he said.

"I gave Cody the medicine." The minute he heard the girl's voice he could tell how distraught she was. "His fever won't go down. And he isn't crying anymore. He's just lying there like a big blob in the bed."

"Is he asleep, Heather?"

"I don't know."

Michael frowned and raked a hand through his hair. He glanced at his watch. Cody's fever should have come down by now—way down. Michael calculated. He could be at the house in twenty minutes.

"Wake Cody and give him a sponge bath. Can you do it? If it frightens you, maybe your mother could come to the house and help." Fear gripped Michael like a vise. Surely, Cody had the flu. But what if this was something else, something much worse? This was one of the downfalls of his profession. For years, he'd been studying worst-case scenarios.

I'm a doctor, he reminded himself. *I've just delivered a baby and prolonged a heart-attack victim's life. Cody won't have any problems I can't deal with.*

He notified them at the nurses' station and headed toward his parking space. Even though it was past 8:00 p.m., it took several minutes for Michael to find a break in the Dallas traffic so he could enter Central Expressway after he'd gotten to his car. He didn't have to change lanes or pass to exceed the speed limit. He sped toward Plano with everyone else, cruising along at over seventy. When he wheeled his car into the driveway, he recognized Heather's mother's car there, too. Inside, he found them both holding Cody in the bathtub, squeezing washcloths of water down his little chest and arms.

"Cody, kiddo, what's wrong?" He stroked his son's hair while his fear escalated. The boy's face was ashen. "Can you tell me if anything hurts?"

"My eyes," Cody whimpered. "And my neck and *everything*."

"Your head? Does your head hurt?"

Cody tried to nod but he winced instead.

"Mostly your neck, though. Huh?"

"Yeah."

Michael bent beside the tub and gathered his son into his arms. He soaked his shirt but he didn't care. Cody tried to smile but he was too weak to move. His eyes lolled backward.

Michael succumbed to his panic. He was no longer the capable physician; he was a frightened father, too afraid to know what to do. "We've got to call an ambulance," he said to Heather's mother. And then he started barking orders at them. "Dial 911 for me. Then give me the receiver." He wasn't going to let Cody out of his arms.

Heather dialed the emergency number and then leaned the phone against Michael's shoulder. He gripped it with his chin. He ordered an ambulance in clipped tones, answered as many of the EMT's questions as he could.

"Dr. Stratton, I'm so sorry," Heather cried when she took the phone from him again. "I don't know what I did wrong."

"You've done a fine job, Heather." He forced himself to reassure the girl. Her round face mirrored the fear he felt himself. "You got your mother here. You got me home to him. And I wasn't so easy to convince, was I?" He moved around the room with his son in his arms, hoping that the air stirring against Cody's wet skin would cool him. The boy felt hot enough to go into convulsions.

Think, he commanded himself. *You've got to examine this child as if he wasn't your own.*

Carefully he propped Cody up on the bathroom counter and studied his face. "Say 'ah,' Cody. Dad needs to see inside your throat."

"Ah-h-h," Cody obliged listlessly. Michael could hardly see anything without his light. What he *could* see looked slightly red but not inflamed. Gently, he bent Cody's neck forward, testing whether he could touch the child's chin to his chest.

Cody cried out.

Michael didn't hesitate when the paramedics arrived. "You'll need a spinal tap and a culture on him," he said. "Have someone from the lab standing by." As they looked askance at him, he realized they didn't know he was a doctor. "I'm a general practitioner," he said. "Where are you taking us?"

"Plano General is closest."

"Just get us there."

As they sped through the traffic it felt like a snail's

pace to Michael. It seemed an eternity before they arrived. After that, things got even worse. He watched helplessly as the paramedics wheeled Cody in on the gurney. An E.R. nurse tried to direct him. "The waiting room is in here, Mr.—"

"It's Dr. Stratton," he said. "I want to stay with him."

"I'm sorry," she said. "You'll have to wait here. You don't have jurisdiction at this hospital."

He didn't answer her. He couldn't. She was right and he knew it. He walked into the waiting room and turned his back to her.

Only then did he realize the mistake he'd made. He let his son's condition terrify him, and he relied on his own wisdom instead of his newfound faith. *Oh Father*, he thought. *I should be praying, shouldn't I?*

Even so, this was the hardest thing he'd had to do in his life, one of the worst things, standing in this waiting room, relying on others to take care of his son. But, just then, he jammed his hands in his pockets, found his BlackBerry, and knew he was wrong. *This* was the hardest thing. He had to phone Jennie.

Jennie Stratton flipped her long mane of blond hair over her shoulder. "So what have we got on Johnson?" She sat atop the stool, her elbow resting on the lighted drawing table, sketching pen in hand, looking down at all of them with a wry grin on her face.

"We've got the fiasco with his neighbor's poodles at

his campaign picnic," somebody volunteered. "We've got his granddaughter arrested for shoplifting earrings from Kmart. And we've got the fact that he told the press it was none of their business when Taylor asked him if he'd ever been treated for alcoholism."

"Has he been treated for alcoholism?" Jennie asked, toying with the idea.

"No. But he still didn't think it was any of our business to ask the question."

This was a dirt-digging session, just like every other, just like every Tuesday night in the press room at the *Dallas Times-Sentinel.* Jennie Stratton was the paper's most infamous political cartoonist. This week the paper would poke fun at three of Texas's most colorful gubernatorial candidates. Jennie plopped both elbows on the drawing table and examined her sketches.

"We'll go with the campaign picnic and the poodles."

"Good choice," someone agreed.

Her cell phone sprang to life on the light table. It almost vibrated itself off the edge. She grabbed it quickly so it wouldn't interrupt the meeting. Why would Michael be calling?

"Hey."

Cody must have forgotten something. He always did. It was so hard for him, living in two houses, two homes, with divorced parents. "What is it? I know it can't be his sneakers. They're in the suitcase underneath his underwear."

"I'm at the hospital," he told her. "I think maybe you should come."

She forgot the editorial staff seated around her. "Michael, what's wrong?"

"Cody's sick. Very sick, Jen. They're running tests."

"What do you think it is?"

"They don't know yet. And I could be wrong."

"Michael?"

He didn't want to say until he was sure. But he knew he owed her this much.

"I suspect meningitis."

For a moment, she didn't speak. Then, "But, Michael, that's something awful, isn't it?"

He didn't mince words. "Yes."

Here came the blame, the same as it had been in their marriage. The suspicion. The hint that he could have done better.

"Has he been feeling badly before today? Has he been complaining about anything you could have treated him for?"

"I would have caught it. I would have seen something, I promise you."

"But he was at your house when it happened."

"He could have been at yours."

"I'm on my way," she said. "Where are you?"

He gave her directions.

"Is there anything you need? Or anything I can

bring from Cody's room to make him feel better? Maybe Mason?"

"I don't need anything," he told her. Then, "Bring Mason. Maybe if he has Mason."

"I will." She snapped the phone shut and turned to her colleagues. "My son is sick. I have to leave."

Then she was out the door and driving like a NASCAR driver toward her house. She ran inside and grabbed a handful of things from Cody's room. Then, for one moment, she stood still, trying to get a grip on reality.

When he'd left yesterday morning, he'd been fine.

Cody had two fully furnished rooms, one at each of their houses, so he didn't have to lug things back and forth when he changed homes every week. He had a set of clothes at each house and a group of his favorite stuffed animals and a Playstation and Legos and almost identical desks where he could do his homework.

Even so, he sometimes forgot important things at one house or the other, his vocabulary workbook or his math problems or his favorite sneakers, and Jennie would drive over and pick them up, or Michael would do likewise. It made Jennie angry sometimes, even while she scolded Cody for being forgetful, thinking of an eight-year-old child living his life being shuffled between two places, between two people who loved him but not each other.

By the time she arrived at the hospital and found Michael, the doctors in E.R. had done the lab work.

Michael took her hand. "I was right, Jen. They've diagnosed meningitis."

His ex-wife stood clutching Mason, the big corduroy brown bunny with a turquoise jacket and neon pink buttons Cody always slept with at her house, hanging on to him as if she were holding on to a lifeline, for herself and for her son.

"Jen. I'm sorry." Michael took her in his arms and hugged her against him. She looked so small and desolate and so much like Cody, with her long blond hair and bangs and her huge, dark frightened eyes. "They're pouring antibiotics into him through an IV."

She was clutching at him, too, with Mason the bunny between them. "Wasn't there something you could have done?"

She's always asking me that, Lord.

Michael shook his head.

"Can I see him?"

"He's in ICU. We get ten minutes every two hours."

"I want him to know Mason's here."

"I want him to know you're here," Michael said.

"Tell me about meningitis," she said, pulling away.

So he did, using a mixture of layman's and doctor's terms, to help her understand it, to do his best to soften the blow. But the details were gruesome. He spoke to Jennie the same way he would inform the mother of any patient who came to him. But Jennie had been his wife once.

He could list a page full of reasons their marriage had

broken up. His hours as an intern at Parkland Hospital. The incredible debt he'd racked up completing med school. Jennie's constant trips to the state capital to search for material for her work. Her low journalist's pay and their arguments about money.

Together, they'd decided to end their marriage four years ago. Neither of them could live a life based on blame. And now, the only thing they shared was Cody.

"Oh, Michael." He could tell she was fighting tears. It seemed a lifetime since he had seen her cry. He didn't think she had even wept during the divorce. Every time he'd seen her in the lawyer's office, her expression had been firm and unyielding, etched as hard as stone.

He cleared his throat before he said, "This'll be rough, Jen." His voice sounded to him like it was coming out of someone else's throat. "Possible blindness. Possible brain damage. We have to wait to see him through it and then count the losses." She sat down hard in the waiting-room chair. "And, if we're lucky, the losses won't include his life."

Just then, the nurse appeared in the doorway. "Are you Cody's mother?"

"Yes."

"You can see him. He's been asking for you."

That was how they spent the next few hours, the two of them taking turns visiting Cody for ten minutes each time a nurse would let them in. It was 3:00 a.m. when Michael went in and Cody clutched his arm. "I'm here, son," Michael whispered over and over again. "I'll always be here for you. Remember that."

"I know, Dad," the little boy whispered. He looked so pale and so small in the starched white bed. Michael felt as if his heart would break, just watching his son, with his eyes, so wide, so innocent, trusting him. Michael's helplessness engulfed him, swallowed him, drowned him. He could do nothing except wait while the deadly bacteria assaulted his son. *Oh Father*, he whispered after Cody had slipped back into unconsciousness. He sank into the chair beside his son's bed and raked both hands through his hair, buried his face in his palms. *Help me to trust You the way my son trusts me.*

Outside, traffic roared past on the highway.

Please, God. I may not have the right to ask for anything. But Cody's so young…he's got his whole life ahead of him.

The monitor beside Cody's bed kept up its steady pace, the peaks and troughs measuring his vital signs.

When he returned to the waiting area, he found Jen waiting for him, sitting in the center of the couch, the tears sparkling like jewels in her eyes.

He touched her arm. "You're exhausted," he told her. "You should sleep."

"I couldn't sleep." She raised her head. Then she shifted on the edge of the sofa, one delicate hand planted on each knee, looking at him. Even though they kept up the facade of friendship for Cody's sake, he knew she was always uncomfortable with him.

"You should try." There were plenty of places to stretch out and rest. But Michael knew Jen well, knew how keyed-up and frantic she could get. "I think you should lie down," he commanded in the same voice he always used. "You're going to need your strength for tomorrow."

At that moment it didn't matter to Michael that they had once caused each other pain…didn't matter that they had loved a lifetime ago and that now it was over. What mattered was that she was woven into the fabric of his life tonight…Jennie…the mother of his son, the son who might not live through the next hours.

During the divorce, they had done everything they knew to make it easier for Cody. But there was nothing they could do to ease what he was facing now.

Chapter Two

By seven the next morning, Cody's condition had stabilized enough that he could be moved by ambulance to Children's Medical Center in Dallas. Jennie and Michael followed the vehicle through the already heavy, early-morning Dallas traffic. Jennie drove her ancient Beemer, weaving it in and out among the cars to keep up. She glanced sideways at Michael when she heard him yawn. He'd taken his glasses off and was rubbing his eyes with his fingers.

"Your turn comes next," she told him. She hesitated, just briefly. "Thanks for the rest, Michael. I needed it."

"Well—" he said "—one of us needed to be lucid today. I figured it might as well be you." The smile faded. "We may have to make decisions."

She stared grimly out through the windshield. "I know that."

When the ambulance pulled up at Children's, Michael and Jennie followed Cody into the building. The waiting rooms were all beginning to look the same. As the morning wore on, Cody's high temperature held and eventually, despite all that the interns did, despite all Michael's prayers, the little boy slipped into a coma. The next time Michael visited him, he could see Cody's hands and legs turning purple and cold from lack of circulation.

He stormed down the hallway to the nurses' station, hoping he was out of Jen's earshot. He might be a high-maintenance father, but he knew too much. He couldn't believe that no one was watching his boy for this. "Get one of the interns," he demanded. It seemed as if hundreds of interns had examined Cody, in groups and individually, every hour. "My son's circulation is stopping. You've got to do something for him."

"We're already on it," the young woman reassured him. "We have a drug we want to try. Something new that might allow circulation."

Michael knew of it. "That could be too strong for him."

"Which is why we're waiting until the treatment is absolutely necessary. We wanted to talk to you and your wife first."

"Not my wife," Michael corrected her. "My ex-wife. We're divorced."

"Does she have custody of the child then?" she asked. "We'll need her consent."

"We have joint custody."

"We'll need both of you to sign the papers. Then explain to her that it's risky but it may be the only chance we have to save your son's legs."

"I'll speak with her," Michael said.

He went back to Jennie and, taking her hand, explained what the doctors wanted to try.

"The medical profession hasn't been able to offer him anything so far that has helped him," he said. *And,* he thought, *neither have I.*

"That doesn't mean we have to stop hoping."

He looked at her then, his eyes full of anguish, surprised she placed faith in medicine when he didn't think he could anymore. Then, drawing on her strength, he nodded. "Okay. We'll give them our consent."

Michael and Jennie stood together, watching, while the doctor administered the first treatment. After that, they had nothing to do but wait. Michael sank back onto the sofa and buried his head in his hands again. Jennie sat beside him, just near enough that he knew she was with him, supporting him. When he finally looked up at her, all of his authority, his mastery, had been swept away. "That's my own son lying there. And I can't do *anything.*"

Jennie knew all too well that marriage didn't always turn out the way it was supposed to. Love didn't overcome every obstacle the way it did in paperback novels. Somewhere along the line, the real world rushed in and took precedence over romance. After a while, romance burned out. Burned out just the same way she and Michael had burned out. Everything…gone. *Except,* she reminded herself, *for Cody.*

She listened to Michael's steady breathing beside her and knew that, at least for the moment, he was getting some rest. She sat perfectly still, not wanting to wake him. It had been four years since she'd seen him like this, so vulnerable and exhausted.

For some unknown reason, her mind traveled to the day she had met him in college. How happy she'd been when he walked over to the huge live-oak tree where she'd been sitting. How happy she'd been when he asked to see her drawings.

He walked by her tree every day with a group of med students going to lab. She remembered glancing up and meeting his eyes. He was tall, with a boyish grin and a headful of thick curls under his baseball cap…broad shoulders…long legs. In fact, she decided he was very nice looking. But what he said next made her think he was cocky, too.

"I know this is nosy but my friends and I have placed a little wager and we would like to know what you do over here under this tree every day."

What a pick-up line, she'd thought.

"These guys think you study every day. But I've bet ten bucks that you're drawing something. Now, if you'd just let me borrow your picture so I can collect my winnings."

"You're pretty sure of yourself, aren't you? Thinking I'll hand my work over to you just like that?"

"Work? That doesn't seem like work to me."

She handed him her sketch pad. "Have a look."

He held it with two hands and looked at it. "Hey! I see these cartoons in the university paper. This is yours?"

She nodded.

"That's great," he said, obviously impressed. "I mean, you're almost famous."

"Almost," she said, laughing. "People don't mob me for autographs yet."

"You're the one who drew all those cartoons last year about the college president taking college funds and going to Cancún?"

"That was me."

"You got him into a lot of trouble."

"I'm good at getting people into trouble," she said.

And that had been invitation enough, it seemed. Just like that, he'd asked her out. He was making a few bucks off of her so she might as well let him spend it on her. They could hang out and have coffee, go to a movie or something.

"You really expect me to fall for that?" she asked him, laughing.

"Well—" he shrugged and then gazed down at her endearingly, like a disappointed little boy "—I thought it was worth a try."

She let him borrow next Monday's cartoon so he

could show it to his waiting classmates. She heard them groaning and then she watched as they all walked away except for him. He brought her sketch back and waggled ten wadded dollar bills in front of her face. "What do you say?"

She couldn't help herself. She'd just kept laughing at him.

"Well, *maybe*."

"That's a committed answer."

"Is that what you're looking for?" she asked. "Commitment?"

But that had been a long time ago.

Jen looked down at him now, down at the huge hand on her knee, the hand had helped heal many. She knew that. This was the very same hand that had taught her so much about being a wife. But being a wife and counting on having a man beside her were two very different things. She knew that, too.

How many times had she longed for Michael when she'd been pregnant when, instead, he'd answered his beeper and been gone for what seemed like days? How many times had she ached for him to say, "You're the most important part of my life, Jen, no matter what other choices I have to make"?

But he hadn't told her that. What's more, she hadn't asked him to. During the six years of their marriage, when he'd been so busy building his practice and his relationship with his patients, she'd been deathly afraid of what he might answer.

It was three the next morning when an intern at Children's Medical Center walked into the waiting room and told Michael and Jen their son was going to make it. Cody's fever had inched down and, without the help of drugs this time, the blood had started easing back into his arms and legs.

At four that morning, the nurse led them into ICU and, with special permission from the doctors, they visited Cody together for the first time. As Jen stooped on one side of the bed and Michael stood behind her, she talked to her son the way she had talked to him when he was an infant and she had held him and offered him the world in her arms. Cody slept through it all. They were both afraid he might still be comatose from the fever. But she said anything that came to mind…crazy things…about Mason and what the stuffed bunny had eaten for breakfast…about the swings in the park he used to play on when he was little…about the snow fort he and his daddy had built during their winter vacation to Steamboat in Colorado.

At her words, Michael's throat constricted with emotion. Jen's quiet, desperate stories reminded him of the family they'd been once, and of the life they'd given Cody. The vacation to Steamboat had been made to salvage their marriage, a last-ditch effort to bring the romance back again when neither of them could understand where it had gone. Actually, he remembered the trip as a disaster. But as he listened to Jen describe the jewel blue day when he and Cody had tunneled into the snow, he remembered other things he hadn't thought of for years: the snowball fight when she'd egged Cody on and his son had walloped him right in the face; catching air with their skis on the moguls high atop Mt. Werner; Jen's face when he'd caught her sneaking up to shove a handful of snow down his collar. To this day, he had to wonder if the vengeful glint in her eye had been from something deeper in her heart than just mischief. That whole trip, she'd seemed intent on paying him back for something.

"Michael," she whispered to him now as she grabbed his hand. "Michael. He's awake."

Cody gazed up at both of them, his eyes narrow with confusion.

"Son," Michael said to him. "Cody. We're here."

Jen stroked hair away from the boy's face. "Yeah, little guy," she whispered. "We're here."

"Hey, Dad…" Then, when Cody saw them beside his bed together, his voice grew stronger. "Mom? What are you doing?"

"Just talking to you."

"What's going on?" Cody asked. He furrowed his brows and tried to raise his head, but couldn't. "Where am I?"

"At the hospital, honey," Jen explained softly. "You've been very sick."

"Did Dad bring me here?" the little boy asked. "Did he take care of me?"

"The ambulance brought you here," Michael told him. "You have other doctors, doctors who knew what to do better than I did…"

Cody gazed up at his father with a worshipful expression. "Nobody knows what to do better than you, Dad."

After Michael left the room to tell someone that Cody had come around, Jen stayed at her son's side. "I brought Mason so he can hang out with you," she said. "He's sitting right over there."

"Where?" Cody tried to prop himself up to see. He couldn't do it.

As Jen watched Cody's futile efforts, a sharp fear began to needle at her. "I'll get him. Don't try to move, Cody. Here." She set the bunny beside his head where he could see it. She began to stroke his hair again as if nothing out of the ordinary had happened.

"I feel really weird, Mom. I wanted to make myself sit up but I couldn't do it."

Her palm hesitated, then continued to smooth his hair back off of his forehead. "Really?"

"How come that's happening? Do you know?"

"I'm not sure."

"It's probably just because I'm sick, huh?"

"Probably," she hedged.

An intern came into the room just then, Michael right

behind him. "Hello, young man," the intern said happily. But that was the last thing Jennie heard. She raced out the door and doubled up against the wall, feeling the anger, the fear, the helplessness as intensely as if it were pounding physical pain.

*No...no...no...*her mind screamed at her. *No... Not my little boy! Not my healthy, perfect little boy...*

"Jen? What is it? What's wrong?"

Michael stood beside her in the hallway. She hadn't even heard him come out of the room. There were only two beings she could blame for her pain just then. Almighty God. And Dr. Michael Stratton.

Michael was the one standing before her. Michael was the one made of flesh and blood. Michael was the one she had grown used to blaming during the years they'd been married.

"Why couldn't you have done something?" she shrieked at him.

He took one step away from her. One step. "I did everything I could, Jennie. You know that."

"I don't know any such thing. I don't know any such thing."

She was crying and he knew she wasn't coherent. But, even so, it didn't make it easier for him. "Don't do this."

"This would never have happened if he'd been at home this week."

"He was at home. He was at home with me."

"Michael, he wasn't *with* you," she shouted. "You

were at the hospital. You're always at the hospital. Why couldn't you have been with him? Why couldn't you have seen it coming?"

Michael clenched his fists, his voice steady. "Where would you have been, Jennie? If this had happened while he was at your house, what would you have been doing? You would have been at the newspaper office. You would have been drawing and having meetings and making plans to blow somebody else's political career sky-high in Austin." There. He'd said it. She ruined people sometimes by what she did, when all he'd been doing was trying to fix them. He'd questioned her motives the entire time they'd been married. He'd told her that, finally, when they were battling for custody of Cody in the Dallas County courtroom. "You wouldn't have seen it coming. You would have been just as helpless as I was."

"I don't know that, Michael," she said coldly. "All I know is that you fought for joint custody and look what's happened. This smacks of negligence. You could have done something if you'd been *with him*."

Here it came again, the same words she said so often. *You could have saved everything if you'd been home.* "Do you think I'm magic because I'm a doctor? Do you think I could have done any more because I have a medical degree and a license to practice?"

"Yes!" she shouted. "Yes, Michael, yes!" It was true. She'd always felt Cody was safer when he was with Michael.

"I'm tired of you holding me responsible for everything," he said quietly as she turned to walk away. "Please don't do this again. Not now."

Jen didn't turn to look back at him. She stalked off and left him standing there, hopeless and alone.

Chapter Three

Andrea Kendall entered the room and read the name on his chart. Cody Stratton. Age: Eight.

She hummed as she flipped through the pages and began to take notes. The interns had called her in on the case early this morning. Mr. Cody Stratton was about to begin the fight of his life.

"Hi," came a bewildered small voice from the bed. "Who are you?"

Andrea could see his eyes peeking out from the bed-covers. "I'm Andrea. Call me Andy."

"Are you a nurse?"

"No. I'm your new physical therapist. I stopped by to take a look at your charts and to meet you."

Cody smiled at that, apparently satisfied. "Good," he said. "This is Mason."

"Has he been sitting here with you ever since you got sick?"

"Yeah. My mom brought him up. He stays at her house usually."

Andrea surveyed the charts once more. She wondered how much Cody knew about his condition. "Has your mother been here this morning?"

"No. I think my dad was here all night. I kept waking up and seeing him over there in the chair. I don't know where he is now."

"Did he talk to you last night after you woke up, Cody? Do you know how sick you were?"

"Yeah," the little boy said. "My dad told me."

She probed further. "What else did he tell you?"

He looked her straight in the eyes. "That I won't be able to use my legs for a while and probably not my arms, either."

She sat down beside him and laid one hand on his leg. His little face was grave. "That's why the doctors want me to work with you, Cody. I've got exercises that will get your arms working again. I've got others that will keep your leg muscles toned."

"Can Mason do them, too?"

"Of course," Andrea said, grinning. "I'll bet he'll be good at it."

There came a knock at the door and the woman who entered was tall and beautiful, her blond hair piled in a fashionable twist atop her head. She nodded to Andy with a smile. "Hello, Cody." She knelt beside the bed. "How's my kid this morning?"

"I'm good." He said it matter-of-factly. The two women in the room knew it was the furthest thing from the truth. But that was okay. It was what Cody thought that mattered.

"How's Mason?"

"He's good, too." Cody glanced at Andrea. "And so's my new friend. That's Andy. My new…"

"Physical therapist," Andrea helped him out, winking at him.

"I'm Cody's mom." She extended a hand. "Jennie Stratton."

Andrea stepped forward to take Jennie's hand. "I'm glad you're here. I need to start working with Cody this morning and I wanted you to be in on it so I can teach you what to do when you get him home. You and your husband are going to have to work just as hard as Cody does."

Jen said sharply. "Cody's father and I are divorced."

"Who does he live with?" Andrea asked. "The parent he lives with will be the parent to administer his therapy."

"He lives with both of us. We have joint custody."

"Eventually, then, your ex-husband—"

Cody interrupted both of them. "Dad was here all night. He slept in that chair." Then, to his mother, "How come you didn't stay, too?"

Jen couldn't answer. She'd left because she'd been exhausted and scared and angry. What had she expected? Michael to come running after her?

The therapist straightened the bedding around the little boy and when she took Cody's hand, she massaged his palms. As she worked, Cody's fingers began to spread apart. Then she took his hand, pushed it flat and straight against her own, so the little boy would bend his elbow. "See," she said, grinning at the bunny. "That's all there is to it, Mason. You can do it, too. What do you think, Cody?"

"I don't know," the little boy told her dubiously.

"I'll never be able to do that," Jen commented.

"You will. Just wait." Andrea continued to manipulate Cody's muscles. "It'll get to be second nature to you. Every time you talk to Cody or do something with him, you just do this a few times. See…watch this."

"What if I hurt him?"

"It'll be painful some days. You can't get around it."

Jennie looked doubtful but she gamely rolled up her sleeves. With a deep breath she turned to her son. "You're sure about this?"

"I'm sure about it," Andrea said.

"I'm sure about it," Cody said.

Andrea held on to Jennie's hand, helping her feel the way it should move against Cody's muscles. "There you go. Look at *that!*"

"*Great,* Mom!" Cody cheered from the pillow.

"Hey," Andy told her. "You're a natural at this."

"Go, Mom!" Cody said, grinning. And with a sinking heart, Jen realized that this was the moment he ought to give her a high-five, only he couldn't.

* * *

Michael stood in the shower, his back against the tile, hot water running down his skin. Every muscle ached from sleeping in that chair. He stuck his head under the steaming water and held his breath. The pain in his muscles began to ease. The pain in his heart did not.

Jennie's words from the night before continued to echo in his head. Just as they'd done all night long.

"Why couldn't you have done something?"

And it turned into a futile prayer. *Dear God, why couldn't I? I have helped so many others, why not my own son?*

He stayed in the shower until the hot water ran out on him. Shivering, he stepped out and toweled himself dry.

He had already telephoned his receptionist and instructed her to cancel his appointments for the rest of the week. A colleague had agreed to take care of emergencies. Michael had nothing left to do except dress and get back to the hospital again.

Jen would be there.

He still knew her, knew how she thought, knew how she struck out in frustration. He'd heard the same words so many times. It seemed she never tired of letting him know how he failed. She never stopped making him question himself.

Why couldn't you have done something? Why couldn't you have been with him? Why couldn't you have seen it coming?

He stood in the center of his Spanish-tiled dressing room and stared into the mirror without seeing. Where had his life gone? What had happened to everything that he'd once held dear?

Negligence, Michael. He heard her voice as clearly as if she'd been in the room with him. He focused on a snapshot of Cody he had taped up above the light where he shaved. A boy in his Little League uniform. There were other pictures, too. Michael's mother and father holding hands at the Honolulu airport. Cody in the bathtub, a pointed beard of bubbles hanging off his chin.

He had taken that one at Christmas. He couldn't remember the year. Maybe 2003. The only thing he knew for certain was that his wife had been there, standing beside Cody just out of the eye of the camera. They'd been playing Santa Claus, trying to make Cody understand, though he was only two years old.

"You look just like Santa," Jen had told Cody as she scooped up another mound of bubbles and let them dribble down his chin. "He's got a long white beard and he's going to come on Christmas Eve and bring you everything you've ever dreamed of."

Everything you've ever dreamed of.

It happens, Michael reminded himself. *Some people get what they dream of. Others, well, they have to go a different direction.*

As Michael stood there measuring the fractions of his life, it honestly surprised him how he'd been able to edit

Jen out. Five years ago, he had thought cutting her out of his life would be impossible. But he was living on his own now, enjoying an occasional dinner date with a lady friend if he ever found the time, this row of glossy photos and three-and-a-half days a week with his son.

Michael yanked a comb through his hair harder than he had intended. He'd already been away from Cody too long. He pulled on a pair of jeans and buttoned his shirt. He looked in the mirror and sighed. A sigh that came from the very depths of his soul.

As Jen watched Andy now, she could tell Cody was exhausted. "Now this," the therapist told him. "Push your hand against my hand. See if you can do it just enough so I can feel the pressure."

"Can't you stop now? He's getting so tired," Jen insisted.

"Let me show you this and then we'll quit. This exercise will make his muscle tone come back. But you must perform it with him at least thirty times each day. Like this..."

Cody groaned at last. "I don't want to do any more. It hurts."

Jen said, "Please don't hurt him."

Andy stopped and stroked back his hair just the way she had seen his mother do it. "It's going to hurt some-times, little guy. And sometimes it might not hurt but it's going to be uncomfortable. I'm sorry. But it's the only thing that's going to make you better." She sat down beside him on the bed. "I've got lots of exciting things planned for you, Cody. In a month or two, you'll be ready to go into a therapy swim program. Water therapy's great. My brother's been working with kids just like you and they have a great time."

Just then, it all sounded too overwhelming for Cody. "I don't want to do all this stuff," he said as big tears began to roll down his little cheeks.

Andy encouraged Cody as best she could. But then, "Hey, kiddo," asked a jovial voice from the doorway. "What's wrong? What are the tears about?"

Jen glanced up to see Michael standing in the doorway. She didn't think she'd ever been so glad to see someone. After all the accusations she'd flung at him he'd stayed the night here, and here he was again, ready to stand beside Cody. She didn't have the time or desire to examine the relief she felt. She just let it spill.

"We're over here learning about therapy," she said. Michael's breath caught a little when he saw how, for the first time, the smile she'd given him went clear to her eyes. "Cody's been doing fine. But he's exhausted now. I'm worried about him."

"Don't get discouraged, Jen."

He read her perfectly. She was surprised he could. But maybe she shouldn't be after the hours they had spent together in the waiting room holding each other up. "I am. Silly, right?"

"No," he said. "Not silly. Just human." He'd counsel any of his patients this way. But because he was telling Jen it meant more.

"Dad." Cody addressed him from the bed. "This is Andy. My new friend. My—" he glanced up at the stranger, trying to remember the right word. This time he did "—physical therapist."

Now Michael saw the cheerful-looking woman waiting quietly on the far side of Cody's bed. "Nice to meet you."

"Likewise." Then, without more preamble, "I'll work with you, too, of course. You'll need to know these exercises since you have joint custody of your son." She made a note on Cody's chart and then she was out the door. "See you tomorrow, Cody."

Cody didn't answer. He was already asleep.

Michael looked at her pointedly. "I see you explained our situation to her." Then, "She worked him hard," Michael said. "What did she tell you?"

"Enough to scare me," she whispered.

"I was afraid of that," he said.

"Yeah," she said. "Me, too."

She gave him a sad little smile. "I wish you didn't know me so well."

For one long, poignant moment, neither of them spoke. Neither of them moved. Neither of them even breathed. They just waited—for what, neither of them knew—matching gaze to gaze. Finally Michael picked up Cody's chart and read it to break the tension. "It would have been harder to go through this alone."

"No," she said. "Nothing can make this harder than it already is."

"Maybe you're right," he commented.

She sounded so certain when she agreed. "I am."

Chapter Four

The therapy swim session had almost ended. Megan, the youngest girl in the group, shivered in her bright red bathing suit as rivulets of water ran down her legs and her crossed arms. Her teeth chattered.

Mark Kendall handed her a towel. "Here you go, kid." He helped her drape it over her head and around her little body. "What's with the goose bumps?"

"The water's c-c-cold…." She pulled the towel so tightly around her that he could see her small, bony shoulder blades jutting through the terry cloth.

"We'll take care of that." He grabbed another towel and started to dab at droplets of water glistening on her arms. "You did great today, Megs."

"You think so?"

"I think so."

Megan grinned.

"Tomorrow we'll get you to swim a little farther."

She wrinkled her nose at him. "I got tired today."

"You can do it, though. I know you can. When you do, you'll be really proud of yourself. Just wait and see."

"You think so?" she asked.

"I think so."

"I'll swim farther tomorrow—" Megan bargained "—if you'll let me get a Pepsi out of the machine today."

He laughed at her. "You sound like Wimpy. 'I will gladly pay you Tuesday for a hamburger today.'"

She looked blank. "Who's Wimpy?"

"You know. Wimpy. On *Popeye*."

Megan still looked lost.

"Oh, great." He slapped his forehead with the heel of his hand. "This girl doesn't know about *Popeye!*"

She clambered up to plop onto his lap. *Along with everything else,* he thought as he winked at her, *I feel old.* "*Popeye* is a cartoon. Where this guy eats spinach and he gets strong and he beats up this bad guy named Brutus."

"It doesn't sound like a very nice story," she said primly. "Beating up people."

"Oh, it's okay." Mark was quick to defend his hero. "He gets the girl, too. A real cute one named Olive Oyl. All because he eats a lot of spinach."

"If I eat lots of spinach, will I get strong?" Megan asked him. "Will I be able to use my arms better so I can swim really fast?"

Mark hugged her. "Nope. It's a nice thought, little

one. But it's all pretend stuff. The only way your arms are going to get stronger is by doing what we're doing. Lots and lots of hard work." Mark glanced up and waved at his sister, who'd just stepped inside the door. Andy waved back.

"Do I get a Pepsi now?" Megan asked.

"Nope," Mark told her. "That's your mom's department, not mine. Here she is, too."

The familiar car had pulled up outside the doorway. Mark saw Megan's mother lean across the front seat to open the door for her daughter. He held the double glass doors open for Megan. "See you next Tuesday," he shouted as the little girl climbed inside the car.

"'Bye, Mark!" Megan hollered back, her little arm fluttering at him outside the window.

He turned inside. Andy was shaking her head. "I can't believe Megan," she commented. "She's doing so well."

Mark began to gather his supplies. "I know." He picked up dented kickboards, several mismatched pairs of water wings and a ball, then pitched them into a plastic laundry basket. "Her arms are getting so much stronger."

Andy tossed one wayward ball in his direction. "I stopped by to tell you I'm going to have a new team member for you soon. I have a new patient. When he gets stronger, I think you can do him a world of good."

Andrea and Mark were as close as twins could be. Their father, George Kendall, had spent his life in a wheelchair after a helicopter crash. Together, Mark and Andy had watched him cope. He'd taught them everything they needed to know about courage, about pushing ahead to tiny victories each day. He was the main reason they'd both grown up to work with patients who needed help.

"You want a hamburger?" Mark grabbed the bundle of folded towels and tucked it under one arm.

Andy shrugged. "Sure." She didn't have anywhere else to go during her lunch hour. "You pick the place. I'll drive."

"You drive and I'll buy." He picked one of his favorite restaurants.

When they arrived, the hostess seated them at a little table for two covered with a red checkered tablecloth. "Onion rings," Mark said, grinning. "It's been ages since I've had onion rings."

"Me, too."

Mark lowered the menu and eyed her. "So...now that I've got you here, how are you *really* doing?"

She screwed up her mouth at him. "Is that what this is? You bring me out for lunch and then interrogate me?"

"I'm not interrogating you. I just want to know."

"I'm fine. Really." She switched to a safer subject. "You'll like the little boy I just started working with at Children's. He's a resilient one. I can tell he's probably going to surprise everyone."

"How old is he?"

"Eight."

"You think he'll beat the odds?"

"The doctors aren't certain yet, but I am."

Mark toasted her with his soda, which he almost felt guilty for drinking after Megan bargaining for Pepsi. "My sister. The person who won't let herself ever expect anything but the happy ending."

"It's the exact way Dad was—" she said quickly, her face softening at the memory. "He always found the good side of things."

Their conversation lulled. Someone flipped a TV on over in the corner and sports scores blared into the restaurant.

"The city council voted down funding for the swim team again," Mark commented offhandedly.

"Oh, Mark, I'm sorry." She leveled her dark eyes on his. What a tremendous blow to him. He'd been working on a proposal for funding for months.

"We'll keep going, I'm sure. The YMCA's said we can use this pool for at least another six months. We need to build a therapy pool that isn't so deep, though."

"I don't know what to say, Mark. You've worked so hard."

"I can get by without new water wings for the kids. The kickboards are disintegrating but those will have to be a second priority, too. I'm going to try to keep the bathing suit fund ready in case I get more kids who can't afford a bathing suit."

"I wish I could do something to help," Andy said, her

words heartfelt. The swim team meant everything to Mark. "Maybe I could take up a collection at the hospital. Or maybe someone would like to donate bathing suits...."

Just as the waitress brought their burgers to the table the TV blared out: "In Major League Soccer action last night, the Dallas Burn lost to the L.A. Galaxy. Even though striker Marshall Townsend found several openings and left forward Chuck Kirkland..."

Someone switched it off.

Great, Mark thought. Just great. *Talk about perfect timing.*

Andy stared at the dark screen, acting as if she hadn't heard the soccer score. But Mark knew she had.

"So," he said, knowing he had to mention Buddy now. "Do you ever hear from him, Andy?"

"No." She turned away from the television to stare down at her hamburger. "He doesn't call."

"The man's a fool."

"No, he isn't. Buddy has his own problems to work through."

"Ahh...and even now you defend him."

She still stared at her hamburger. "Yes. I guess I do."

"Does he deserve that, Andy?"

"I was pretty hard on him, Mark." She met her brother's gaze at last. "It's tough reasoning with a therapy patient when you're emotionally involved. A lot of it was my fault."

"What did you say to him?" Mark asked.

Andy sat back in her chair and let her mind wander. What did I say to Buddy? What *didn't* I say to Buddy?

During the past year, she'd gotten used to the thought that she'd always be a part of Buddy Draper's life. They'd met at a New Year's Eve party, laughing and throwing confetti and cheering as the clock struck midnight.

"You've got stuff in your hair," he'd told her as he picked a swirl of paper off the top of her head. Everyone around them was kissing and singing "Auld Lang Syne." It was the first time she'd ever laid eyes on him. Yet, still, he seemed vaguely familiar.

"Everybody has stuff in their hair," she'd said, trying unsuccessfully to come up with something witty to say. "It's midnight on New Year's Eve."

She extended her hand gracefully. "Happy New Year, Mr.—"

"Draper. Buddy Draper."

A slight pause. She'd figured out later he'd been waiting for her to recognize his name. But she hadn't.

She introduced herself, too, and they'd shaken hands. Then they'd laughed and exchanged pleasantries for another half hour, he'd said several things about this "calling" that led her to believe he might be a Christian. Oh, how she'd hoped he was, as she'd gathered her belongings and had taken her keys out of her purse.

"I'll take you home," he suggested.

"No," she said. "I just met you. That would never do." Even so, she was pleased that he'd offered.

Early the next morning he phoned her and asked if she wanted to go to the Cotton Bowl parade with him.

"This is crazy," she said, sitting straight up in bed and holding the receiver with both hands.

"It isn't crazy. The parade starts up Commerce Street in an hour. You could be there."

"It'll be hard to find a place to stand coming that late."

"I bet you'll be surprised," he told her. "We'll find a place."

"I guess we could," she said, still clutching the receiver, with a fluttering in her stomach that made her feel like she was in high school again.

An hour later she gasped as they climbed the steps to the grandstand and Buddy pulled out a metal chair for her beside the mayor of Dallas.

"Why are *we* up here?" she whispered to him after she'd been introduced to half the public officials in Dallas.

He crossed his arms and stretched out his feet. "We're here because this is where I always sit."

It wasn't until the J. J. Pearce High School Marching Band tromped by playing *Spirit in the Sky*, halfway through the parade, that he offhandedly mentioned he played soccer.

"That's what you do for a living?"

"Yeah," he said, chuckling. "At least it was last time

I looked. But maybe I'd better check again. I might be an insurance salesman now."

That's when it all started piecing together in her mind and making sense, the name, the vaguely familiar, handsome face, the seats of honor they occupied. "You play for the Burn," she said in a whisper. "You're Buddy Draper."

He didn't look at her. He just took her hand. "I thought I told you that last night."

After the day of the parade, they did a lot of things together. They rode bumper cars and wandered around a flea market. They attended a film festival together. She invited him to visit her church one Sunday and he did so readily, promising he'd invite her to join him for services at the non-denominational worship center he attended. After that, Andy's priorities had shifted. She loved her patients and urged them forward. But, now, with Buddy in her life, her patients weren't the compelling force that drove her soul any longer. Buddy took over a new, special corner of her heart. The two of them spent quiet time alone together every weekend. He gave her tickets to every Dallas home game. She sat with the other players' girlfriends or wives and cheered him on.

She wasn't certain she loved him until one afternoon when the Burn played in San Jose. The Earthquake defeated them in California. She drove to Dallas/Fort Worth International to meet the plane and, when she went to the charter gate, there was a crowd of people waiting to greet the team when they came in.

Just before the plane landed, a security guard came up behind her and took her by the arm. "You Andy Kendall? We're bringing the plane into a hangar away from the terminal. Those players are exhausted and Harv Siskell doesn't want them to have to face this crowd right now. We've got all the wives boarding a shuttle. Liza Townsend saw you standing here and thought I should let you know."

"Thank you," she said quietly, following him. The shuttle bounced across the tarmac and they disembarked inside the cavernous hangar, huddling in a group as the jet pulled inside, too.

Liza Townsend's husband, Marshall, was a striker on the team like Buddy. She held their little boy in her arms while he squirmed. He was ready for bed, dressed in a fuzzy blue blanket sleeper. And, as the steps went up and the players started to climb down, Marshall Townsend was one of the first off the plane. Liza set the little boy on the floor and he ran to his father, squealing with delight, arms outstretched.

No defeat would be that bad if you had a child to greet you, Andy thought. So here was the real portrait of life for these players. It had nothing to do with what happened on the soccer field. It had everything to do with reunions and families and belonging to each other. As Andy saw Buddy starting down the metal stairs, looking disheveled and exhausted, she felt a strong sense that God meant her to spend her life with Buddy, that this man could be 'the one.'

She met him at the bottom of the steps and he wrapped his arms around her.

"Hi," she said.

"Boy, am I glad to see you," he said, right before he kissed her.

"Interesting spot to meet an incoming flight," she commented, teasing him.

"Was there a crowd in the terminal?"

"Yes. A big one."

"Thanks for dealing with all this."

She gazed up at him. "Buddy. I…" But she stopped, shy. This wasn't the place or the time to tell him how he made everything worth it, how she felt like the Lord might be leading them to something more.

"What?"

"Nothing."

"No. Tell me. What?"

"I missed you, is all."

"Good," he said. "I wanted you to miss me. That's the only way I survived the end of that game, knowing I was going to get on a plane and fly back here to you."

"It was a good game, Buddy. You didn't embarrass yourselves."

"We didn't win, either."

"In my eyes, you won."

"You're prejudiced."

"Isn't everybody?"

"No. Just you."

She laughed, a light tinkling sound that seemed to waft up and hang in the air above them. She pulled her keys out of her purse. "Here. I'm the chauffeur for the evening."

"Good," he said, grinning, but his eyes showed how exhausted he was. When they arrived at his house, they lay on the floor listening to Mendelssohn, Andy's chin propped on her palm, while Buddy talked about the game. He fell asleep on the floor and, before she left, she covered him with an afghan he usually kept spread across an armchair. She kissed him once on the forehead then gazed down at his sleeping face, figuring that the next time she saw him she'd tell him how much she loved him.

It was the last time she saw him before the accident.

She drove home to her apartment and went to bed. The next afternoon, when she finished with her patients in the gym and went to check her messages, the call from Harv Siskell had come in. She'd driven like a maniac all the way to the hospital. When she got there, they told her he was in intensive care and no one could see him except immediate family. Four days and four sleepless nights later, he moved to a private room and she finally got to see him.

"I wrecked my car," he told her as she stooped beside his bed.

"I know that."

"I wrecked my legs, too."

"So I hear."

"Oh, Andy," he whispered to her. "What am I going to do? I've got to play soccer again. It's my calling. It's the only thing I've ever wanted to do."

"You'll play again," she promised, taking it to heart. "I know just what to do."

For months he went to physical therapy as an outpatient at Parkland Hospital. For months Andy pushed him even further. They worked in the gym at Children's for what seemed like an eternity. As Andy expected, it paid off. Buddy walked again. He ran again. Just not as fast as he'd run before. And he couldn't run as far. When the Burn assessed him for the next season, he wasn't nearly as certain of himself anymore.

"Well," he said as he sat down on Andy's sofa one evening. "I made a decision today."

"About what?" She came around the arm and handed him her favorite healthy concoction, a drink blended from cantaloupes and bananas.

"I told Harv this morning I'm going to retire."

She'd stopped in mid-sip of her own drink and eyed him as if she were eying a stranger. "Buddy. No. You can't."

"I have to, Andy. It's the only choice I could make."

"It isn't." Then fiercely. "It isn't at all."

She couldn't believe it. As she watched him sitting not quite so complacently now beside her, all she could think of were his desperate words from not so very long before.

It's my calling.

"You can't do this," she said softly, hoping the low volume of her voice would cover the frustration she was feeling, only it didn't. "Why would you stop like this if soccer is something you're so passionate about?" She had seen so many children fight so much harder to get their lives back. "You haven't even *tried* yet."

He stood and glared at her. "Why do you say that? What do you know about what I'm feeling? You don't want me this way, is that it?" She knew what he was thinking, but it made no difference. "You don't want me. I'm not a professional soccer player, is that it?" This must have happened to him all too often before; women agreed to go out with him because he was a celebrity. And now he was obviously thinking she was no different from the others.

"You've got it wrong, Buddy. I'm against this because of how much you wanted it, because of how hard you worked to come back. Because of how hard *we* worked…"

"Tell me something." His eyes were cold. "Did we spend all those evenings in that gym for *me* or for *you?*"

"You tell *me* something," she shot right back at him. "You told me that soccer is your *calling.* Does your calling come from yourself, or does it come from God?"

"Now, that's between me and God, isn't it?"

"You were happy, weren't you, Buddy? You were happy as long as the goals and the fame came easy for you. But now that you won't be the star player anymore, now that you won't make so many goals, now that you're going to have to work for it, you *give up*. I think you've decided to take the easy way..."

She faded out. She didn't know what else she could say to him. It was impossible for her to watch him surrendering and not be angry about it. So maybe he wouldn't be the best-loved player on the team anymore. But at least he'd be doing what he wanted to *do*. After all the work she'd done with children who might not ever be able to walk again, she couldn't believe he was standing before her now, a whole man, telling her he was backing away. "Anything I ever did for you—" she told him now in a quavering voice "—was because I loved you."

There. She'd said it, after so many months. But she'd said it much, much too late for both of them. "All the kids I've watched fighting for their dreams, Buddy. I never thought that you would be the coward."

"Andy," he said, his voice pleading now as he draped his jacket over his arm. "Don't judge me by this. Unless you've played the game, you don't realize when you're running out of options."

"I've played plenty of games," she said, tears streaming down her face as he stepped past her toward the door. "And I'm tired of them. It just isn't in me to let somebody give up."

That had been almost six months ago. Andy hadn't

seen or heard from Buddy since. Her life was empty again except for her brother, Mark, and the caseload of children that kept her busy at Children's Medical Center.

"All right!" Andy urged the little girl on. "Let's see turtle legs kicking…kicking…" She clapped her hands for the little girl who played beside her on the pallet. "That's what I like to see." She turned to the two parents sitting beside her, watching. "I can tell you've been working with her at home."

"We have been," the proud father told her. "Every day. All the time."

Andy motioned for the candy striper to bring her a towel from the cabinet. "Let's try something new. Challenge time, kiddo." Andy rolled the towel and placed it beneath the eighteen-month-old's stomach. She showed Kara how to place her arms to balance herself. Then she dug around in the toy bin.

"Let's see what we can find that's interesting in here."

Andy pulled out a tin funnel, its rim lined with holes and metal rings and six different sizes of measuring spoons.

Kara squealed and reached for them as they jangled.

The little girl flopped over against the towel and rolled off it.

"Oops." The therapist caught Kara and laid her on the rolled towel again. "Let's try again."

Kara reached over and over again for the jangling

spoons. And over and over again, she toppled off the mount Andy had made for her.

"She's right where she needs to be." Andy reassured the parents every time she reached out to catch the child. "This will start to get easier. She's a fast learner."

Andy stared out the window for a moment, her fingers cupping her chin, trying to remember her schedule. "When's your next appointment with Kara's doctor?"

"Two weeks from Friday," they said together.

"I'd like to see her before then." But she caught the worry on Kara's mother's face immediately.

"Is that a problem?"

"We won't have enough for the train fare that soon," Kara's father admitted.

"I'll make an appointment for the same day she'll see the doctor, then. You can bring her for therapy when you're already here."

"That would be better. Maybe next month we can bring her in more often."

It was the most painful thing Andy could think of, a child who needed therapy but who couldn't get it as often as needed. She understood her brother's financial frustrations so well. In many ways, they were her own.

Children's Medical Center charged its patients based on their ability to pay. But what about the children like Kara whose parents couldn't afford the train fare to bring her in? It was for that very reason that Mark had established his bathing suit fund. For some of Mark's water therapy patients, a new bathing suit was as unattainable as a new house.

The other kids didn't know how lucky they were. Kids like Cody Stratton whose parents would be able and willing to give him anything…everything…to make him well again.

Others, like Buddy Draper, could buy the moon and it still wouldn't be enough.

Father, Buddy is out of my life, she prayed. *I thought I knew Your will. I thought it was safe to give my heart.*

Chapter Five

Buddy Draper plopped his loafer-clad feet atop his desk and leaned back to watch the game video for the third time. He groaned as he watched Townsend struggle to catch up with the ball. He shook his head as he noted the point where the man gave up and began falling back.

I never would have played it that way, he thought. *If I had been playing full throttle I never would have given up.*

Andy's long-ago words echoed in his head. *You were happy being the celebrity soccer player as long as the goals and the fame came easy for you. But now that you won't be the star player anymore...now that you won't make so many goals...now that you're going to have to work for it, you give up.* How dare she compare him with those kids she worked with. This was his *career.* This was different. She'd told him, *I never thought that you would be the coward.*

As Buddy watched his friend and former colleague pull up behind the ball, he heard the roar of the crowd in his ears again, remembering what it felt like to run across the indoor field in pursuit of a ball rolling so fast it was only a blur sometimes, while his fans roared.

He reminded himself, *It wouldn't ever be the same.*

The phone call he'd received this morning had taken him by surprise. He had been away from the field for so long now that he thought most people had probably forgotten he ever played.

"Buddy," Harv Siskell had boomed at him over the line. "I'm sending a courier over with tapes. I want you to have a look at them and tell me why we didn't win last night." Harv had been coaching Buddy since he'd been a sophomore at Southern Methodist.

"Why does it matter what I think?" Buddy asked him brusquely.

"Because I need a new assistant coach!" Harv bellowed at him. "I want to know what's wrong with my game. Then I'll tell you what's right about your input."

"Suppose I'm not interested in viewing your tapes?"

"Too late, Buddy. They're already on their way. And, Bud…"

"Yes?"

"Don't worry about tipping the courier. He's my nephew. He was drooling buckets just to ring your front doorbell and have a look at you."

"Thanks, Harv." His tone said, *Thanks for nothing.*

"Call me as soon as you've got comments for me."

Even with the advance notice, Buddy jumped at the knocking on his door a few minutes later.

"Gee, Mr. Draper...Buddy..." the boy said, stumbling in his excitement. "It's great to meet me...I mean, meet you!" He held the package out to Buddy. "My uncle sent these over. He told me I could bring them."

Buddy took the package and handed the little boy a dollar bill. "Thanks, son."

The kid never even noticed the tip. He just kept staring at Buddy. "I'm in the fourth grade at Prairie Creek Elementary School in Richardson. We play soccer every Saturday. I've been playing since I was five years old and I practice all the time."

"That's what it takes," Buddy said, standing there holding the door open and waiting for the boy to leave, for no good reason deciding he was in a hurry now to tear open the packet and watch the game. "It takes hard work and practice...for all your life..."

"That's what my uncle says, too. He got us all tickets to the last three Burn games. He can get them for us anytime we want."

The boy just stared up at him, his brown eyes huge and glowing.

"That's really nice," Buddy said, touched.

"Oh, gee, Mr. Draper...Buddy...would you mind...? I mean, if you've got time...I really wanted..."

"Yes, son?"

"I really wanted…your autograph?"

Buddy grinned. It had been months since anybody had asked him to sign anything. "Sure thing, kid."

"I thought about you signing my soccer ball but it gets kicked around so much that I knew it would rub off. You don't mind writing on paper, do you?"

Buddy invited the boy in. His eager guest followed him as he pulled a Sharpie out of his drawer and fished around in the closet for a team sweatshirt. "Here," he said when he found it. "Now. What's your name, son?"

"Billy," he said. "Billy Siskell."

Buddy hated to admit it but he felt better than he'd felt in a long time. He looked at the little boy again. "B-I-L-L-Y? I want to be sure I spell it right."

"That's right," Billy told him.

"To Billy Siskell," he wrote, "an excellent courier and soccer player. Keep on kickin'. Buddy Draper. The Dallas Burn."

It wasn't until he'd scribbled the last part of it that he realized he couldn't officially write "The Dallas Burn" beneath his name anymore.

He handed Billy Siskell the sweatshirt and Billy clutched it to his chest. "Thank you, Mr. Draper. Thank you for the shirt!" The boy reached over and pumped his hand, trying very hard to be a man. "Thank you."

"You're welcome, Billy."

Then Buddy stood, smiling now, genuinely smiling, watching the kid pick his bike up out of the grass and ride away.

* * *

Exactly ten days had gone by since Cody had gotten sick. When Jennie Stratton arrived at her office at the *Dallas Times-Sentinel* this morning, she felt oddly out of place. It startled her that everything could go on as usual, day in and day out, despite what had happened to her son. Reporters clacked away on the computer keyboards and the phones were ringing off the hook in the newsroom. She felt as if she'd stepped outside herself and were watching everything from some vast distance.

Someone spoke to her. "We're so sorry about your little boy." She wished people didn't think they had to say things. It would be much easier if she didn't have to respond.

"Thank you," she said. "It's been very hard."

She made her way up the stairs to Art Sanderson's office. In one hand, she clutched the portfolio containing cartoon sketches she hadn't worked on in days.

Her editor met her at the top of the stairway. "Our sympathies, Jen. We're sorry about Cody."

"The flowers were lovely, Art." The staff had sent a huge bouquet to Cody's room at Children's, big purple carnations and yellow mums, topped off with a half dozen balloons. Cody had loved the balloons, of course.

"You up for a staff meeting?" Art asked her. "I'd like to bring you up to speed on what everyone's doing. We had to go ahead and make decisions about the gubernatorial series."

"That's fine."

"We made the decisions in a pinch. We hated doing it without you."

"You'd better call everyone together and fill me in."

She could tell by the guarded pleasure in Art's eyes that he was impressed she'd returned to work so soon after Cody had taken ill. Which was fine. He ought to be. She *was* going beyond the call of duty. But she was doing it for herself, not for anyone else.

I have to do something to keep from hurting. Only it never stops.

Jen went to her own desk and sifted through the papers. She flipped through several rough sketches to remind herself what she'd been working on. She jotted down several notes to herself and was in the middle of organizing them when a thin young man with unruly hair stuck his head in the door. "Jen! Hello! I've been trying to call you for days."

"I haven't been home much, Kirby. I've been at the hospital with Cody."

"I haven't seen you looking this exhausted since you were going through the divorce."

She flipped a pen at him. Kirby had been the entertainment editor at the *Times-Sentinel* for years, an aging dancer who had long since retired from the Dallas Metropolitan Ballet and turned to reviewing performances instead. He had proven a loyal friend over the past years. "It's good to see you, too."

"I've been worried about you."

"Everybody's been worried about me." She smiled; she appreciated his concern. Just talking to Kirby helped her get a little of her spunk back.

"Has it been tough spending time with Michael?" he asked.

She sighed. "I haven't had time to think about it," she answered honestly. "This has been a lot more traumatic than anything I've gone through before."

Kirby sat on her desk. "You've forgotten, I think. Your divorce from Michael was pretty traumatic. All those days you could hardly work because you were so upset. And what about the night you waited up for him until three in the morning to come home from the hospital?"

"Kirby…"

"He didn't deny that, did he?"

"There is nothing," Jen said quietly, "more traumatic then thinking you might lose a child."

"What about the day he came storming in here waving your latest cartoon at you and accusing you of ruining Buzz Stephens's career? That man ruined his career all by himself, Jen. You just drew a cartoon about it."

"Kirby, Michael and I made a career of accusing each other of things. We're still doing it. I don't want to talk about this right now." For some reason, she felt as if she were betraying a close friend by rehashing all of this today. Michael had just helped her too much during the past days. They had to stand strong together because of Cody. He didn't deserve this from her now.

She gathered up her things and walked down the hallway with Kirby to the meeting. She perched on the stool at the drawing table, her usual spot, and called them all to order. "Okay," she said, and it struck her as bizarre just then, that this was just where she'd been sitting, these were just the people she'd been talking to, when her world had turned upside down. "Tell me what we're doing. Art says he doesn't know if I'll like it."

"We had to trash the idea about the poodles at the picnic," one of the artists told her. "Art thought that, by the time you could get it drawn, it wouldn't be relevant anymore. He wants us to go with an entire series about—" he hesitated almost imperceptibly, but it made Jen steel herself for what was coming. Something was up "—the Texas politicians who are having affairs. Art thinks it'll be a nice satire, something they might even pick up for *Texas Monthly*." The other heads around the table nodded in agreement.

"No." She shook her head. "No…no…no." It was all so incredibly stupid and trivial. She tried to remember when political satire had meant something to her. Certainly it had. But no more. "I'll talk to Art about it. Don't do anything yet."

They went on to other things. At the end of the meeting, Jen sat feeling incapable and out of touch while her entire staff filed by her, chattering. Her meeting with

Art later wasn't much better. "We've done too *much* of that," she told him, referring to the "Adulterous politician series," as she'd started to think of it. "I wanted something creative. I wanted something that would make people laugh instead of saying, 'Oh, no, not again.'"

"You've got to go with me on this one. We don't have time for anything else."

"I hate it," she said matter-of-factly, jumping up off the chair and prowling around like a cat, her hair hanging in a gold sheath down her back.

"I did the best I could without you." Art leaned back in his chair. "I'm not going to change it now."

So that's where it ended. Jen returned to the artists that afternoon and told them to start working where they'd left off. Everyone knew she'd been overruled.

Michael and Jennie had just come from a visit with Cody, and had left him fast asleep.

"It was a mistake, going to work today," she told Michael. "I thought it would help me forget for a few hours. But nothing helped."

"I'm still not seeing patients. I couldn't have diagnosed a child this week if the President of the United States had brought one in. Russell's covering for me until further notice."

She looked up at him, surprised he was referring all his patients to someone else. When they had been married, he'd never done that.

Her gray eyes were huge. And her questions were telling, filling him with questions of his own. "We're good parents, aren't we?" she asked.

They looked at each other wordlessly.

When they reached the lobby of the hospital, Jennie didn't want to say goodbye to Michael just yet. She needed to be near him, just as she had needed him for the past few days. She needed not to be alone now.

"You want to go get something to eat?" she asked. He didn't even hesitate before he nodded. He must have felt the same way. Together they walked to the cafeteria. They both bought sodas and hamburgers wrapped in greasy paper. Then they sat down at a table and sipped their drinks. For an eternity, neither of them spoke.

Then, as if he wanted to break the silence he said, "I've got an answer to your question."

"What question?"

"Whether we're good parents."

She bit into her hamburger, wiped mustard off her lips with the napkin.

"Remember when I was serving my internship at Parkland and Cody was teething?"

She thought back, then grinned. "Oh, I remember that, you mean when his bottom ones were coming in?"

He nodded, smiling for perhaps the first time in days. "The first tooth. You brought him into the hospital at three in the morning so I could get a look at it."

"You think that was funny?" She couldn't resist teasing him just a bit. During their married life together, they'd jousted often. "It was better than sitting there on the sofa with him, listening to him cry all night long. Riding in the car always made him feel better. So we rode in the car and came to see you."

"I thought that was quite the accomplishment, him getting that tooth."

"Yes," she agreed. "You were so proud. I remember you showed it to every doctor doing night duty at Parkland."

"They were all so impressed, too."

"Oh, I'm sure they were," she said, tilting her head at him and laughing. "I'm sure they'd never seen anything like it before in their lives."

That was back in the days when I thought I could perform miracles, Michael thought. "I thought that tooth was the coolest thing." Then he chuckled. "You know, they always say doctors make the craziest parents. We're even more amazed by all our kids' feats than other people."

"You certainly were."

Silence came between them again. It lasted a long time.

"We were good parents, Jen. Maybe crazy sometimes, but good. You were a good mother. You still are."

She plopped her elbows on the table, chin in palms, surveying his features, honestly surprised at his words. Honestly surprised at how comfortable she felt with him. His face was familiar to her yet it was different, too, with wrinkles at the corners of his eyes where wrinkles hadn't been before, deep lines around his mouth that spoke of his concern for his patients and of his painstaking work.

Their eyes met. She looked sad. "I just wasn't a very good wife."

He didn't answer. Lots of water had gone under the bridge. There are always two sides to everything. And it didn't really matter because it hadn't been her fault. They had both decided, a long time ago, that it would have been better if they hadn't married one another in the first place. Each of them had been sailing in a separate direction, seeking dreams and a life, each of them unavailable when the other needed support. They'd both been very, very young.

He fingered his paper cup. "Those days don't matter anymore, do they?"

She shook her head. She didn't know what she could say. And then she looked up at him again. "Yes. I think they do matter. We had some good times together. We both got Cody out of it. They matter because they remind us that neither one of us was to blame."

"Or that both of us were."

The silence came again.

"Come on," he said finally, laying two quarters on the table for the busboy who was mopping tables with a rag. "Time to go home."

She pulled on her jacket and heaved her bag over one

shoulder and walked beside him, still quiet. At last, just as they arrived in the lobby, she touched his arm to stop him.

"What is it, Jen?"

"I blamed you for this, Michael. I blamed you for everything that's happened to Cody."

"Yes," he said. "I know that."

She had to say the rest of it. She knew him so well from so long ago. And she could see it in his eyes. "And *you* are blaming yourself, too."

He stared straight ahead, out the plate-glass window toward the parking lot.

"There isn't anything you could have done."

He glanced at her, acknowledging her absolution but knowing it wasn't going to be that easy for him to accept forgiveness. He let her lead him to a row of chrome chairs lining the wall. They sat.

"I had to blame somebody, Michael. And you were the one who was there, flesh and blood, standing in the room with me."

"Do you know what I would give," he asked, "if there had been something…anything…I could have done for him?" He stared at the ceiling, at the splotchy drywall there, seeing only his son's little body and the baby-sitter's frightened face when he rushed in from the hospital to them. "I would die myself if I could trade that for what's happening to him. I ought to have been able to see it, to stop it."

"Some things just happen."

"I don't know about that."

"I'll always have questions about this," she told him softly. "But they won't be questioning your abilities. I have faith in everything you did for him, Michael."

He gripped her hand and looked at her for the first time in long minutes. "Will you, Jennie? Will you have faith in what I have done? In what I didn't do?"

He was such a strong man one moment, more vulnerable than she'd ever seen him the next. Without even thinking, she went to him, to let him hold her when he held out his arms. "Michael." She stroked his hair the way she would have stroked it every night if only he'd been able to stay beside her, if only he hadn't always been called to duty at the hospital. If only she hadn't been so young when they'd married. If only she could have understood then what he had to do.

Chapter Six

Cody Stratton knew exactly when Andy was going to come in every day. He loved to hide from her and make her laugh. He'd groan when he saw her opening the door and then he'd do his best to burrow down into the covers so she couldn't find him.

"Guess where I am," he'd say, doing his best not to giggle. But she always found him no matter what he tried. Then, after she did, it was always the same, up and down…up and down…up and down…his knees and legs folding up accordion-style against his belly while she worked with him.

"Now. You do this at least three times a day," Andy always told his mother. "You've got to work at this to keep him from getting so stiff. When you work with his hands, you want to move your fingers in a circular motion like this, relaxing his fingers apart instead of prying them. When you stretch his neck, you want to move it in a circular motion, too, like this...."

Cody's mom always wrote everything down. There was no way she could remember all this stuff if she didn't. At least, he didn't think so.

"I just realized," she said once to Andy while Cody watched her, "you don't give any review questions. You just plow into something new every time I see you."

"When you're working with his elbows, you want to rotate the movement just this way...." Andy kept right on going.

"Hey," Cody said to both of them. "This isn't fair, y'all. All Mom has to do is write down the stuff. But I'm the one who has to *do* all the stuff."

"You!" His mom bent down close to him and kissed his nose. "You're doing a *great* job! You're doing the hardest work of all and we know it."

Cody loved the way his mom smelled, like roses and outside. Andy smelled good, too, but his mother was special. He loved the way she told him he was doing his hardest work. And, best of all, he loved it when she cuddled with him now, though he knew he was getting much too old to admit that.

"You're getting your tone back in your arms," Andy told him. "It won't be long before you're *swimming*."

"Yeah." Swimming sounded like the best thing in the world after lying in bed for so long. He listened while she told him all about her brother Mark and what he did with kids in the water. She told him about a little girl named Megan and how working in the water had helped her to be able to use her legs again. All the while Andy kept working on him and moving his arms every which way while his mom took enough notes to fill a book.

He was the first one to see his dad standing in the doorway looking at his mom. "Hi, Dad!" he hollered so loud he made his mom jump. "Dad's here!"

"Hello, kid." His dad walked straight to the bed and gave him a hug. Cody knew his dad was pretending that he'd just gotten there. He wondered how long his father had been standing at the door watching them.

"You're sweating," his dad said.

"That's because I'm doing therapy."

"And doing a good job of it," Andy said as she laid his leg down and covered it with the blanket. "He's doing great moving his arms. They're loosening up nicely." She touched him lightly on the nose. "Time for a break now, kiddo."

"I get to go to the therapy gym tomorrow," Cody told his dad. "It'll be my first time."

"Good for you." And, for a moment, because his dad hesitated, Cody thought that he might not know what to say. "...I think that's great. I wouldn't expect a patient to do as well as you've been doing." He bent over the bed and gave Cody several well-placed tickles right on the ribs as Cody rolled onto his side in a fit of giggles. "Stop doing so good! You're doing too good!"

"I can't *help* it," Cody squealed. "It's just happening."

* * *

Jennie sat and watched her sleeping child for a moment, watching the flicker of lashes on his slightly flushed cheeks and the rise and fall of his small chest. "He's doing so much better than they thought he would," she said after a long silence. "Thank heaven for every breath that little boy takes."

"Do you really mean that?" Michael asked, because it suddenly seemed important to know where she was coming from. Was she really thanking heaven? He didn't know if she'd ever have much trust in God.

He searched Jennie's face, thinking how different his ex-wife looked. Their eyes met and held.

"So," he asked at last. "How, exactly, do you go about learning all this?"

"I've got outlines of the therapies we're supposed to do with him when we get him home. Or—" she corrected herself, realizing what she'd said "—when *I* get him home…and *you* get him home. I'll never remember all this stuff if I don't take notes."

Michael swallowed. Hard. Just looking at her he felt off-center. All he wanted to do lately was be around his ex-wife and do things for Cody. "You want to show me those notes? Are you up for another cafeteria hamburger?"

She almost said yes. But then she allowed a slow smile to lift the corners of her mouth. "You want the truth? The *real* truth?"

He grinned, too, a warm, full smile that made her

heart feel as if it were flopping in somersaults. "Say no more. I don't want to hear the truth, that you'd like to go down to the cafeteria and slaughter every single one of those hamburgers with a shotgun."

"Okay. I won't say it."

"That's it, then." He stood and helped her up. He had half a mind to suggest they eat out somewhere. But, calculating the days since he had last eaten a home-cooked meal, he said instead, "Let me cook something for you."

At the mention of a meal at a real table with real forks and glasses instead of paper cups, Jen's eyes widened. "It sounds like paradise."

"Come on," he said. "Let's do it."

He drove her in his car, all the while intensely aware of her sitting beside him, her hands folded neatly in her lap, her eyes cast upward through the sunroof. It seemed like forever since they'd driven along together like this, even longer since the two had cared what was happening in each other's life. For one brief, insane minute, Michael found himself wishing he could reach across the front seat and take her hand.

But they'd been married once and it would mean too much. He concentrated on the expressway, both hands gripping the steering wheel. He could think of nothing to say.

Finally they pulled into the driveway at his house. The garage door rolled open for him. He fumbled with the house key, displaying nerves. She followed him into the house carefully, holding her handbag in front of her. He strode into the kitchen and started rummaging through the refrigerator. "Look what we've got here. Moldy peas. Some macaroni and cheese wrapped in a Baggie. Half of an overripe cantaloupe."

"Very appetizing," she teased. "If you really want to know the truth—" she told him candidly "—it *still* looks better than the cafeteria hamburgers."

"Trust me," he said, shooting her a little grin. "I'm going to find something that's edible. It'll just take a minute." He poked his head farther into the fridge.

"Don't let anything attack you in there. Some of it looks deadly."

"This is it. Here. I've got it." He pitched out an unopened package of flour tortillas, a tomato, a head of lettuce that was a little wilted but would do, and some salsa. "I've got chicken in the freezer and I can defrost it. We'll have *fajitas.* It won't take long."

"Thank you," she said, laughing. "I would have killed you if you had gotten my hopes up for nothing."

They set to work, side by side. She chopped the lettuce into little strips and diced the tomato while Michael took care of everything else. She didn't look up when she heard him go out onto the patio to start the grill.

Now that he wasn't standing within feet of her, she contemplated how odd it felt to be cooking with Michael in his kitchen. It felt right. And wrong. And funny.

Michael wandered back inside looking for a match to light the grill.

Jennie dissected the tomato perfectly, paying close attention to the little squares she made, trying to ignore her response to Michael's presence. After almost two weeks spent discussing Cody, she couldn't think of one thing to say.

"I had to get the matches," he said. "Can't start a fire out there if I can't find the matches." For a moment he just stood there, watching her with her head bowed over the tomato and all the wheat-colored hair flowing down her back. Then, as if in a vision, a memory came back.

It had been their first night in their tiny apartment in Highland Park. He'd come home to find her standing much as she was standing now, her long sheet of hair gleaming down her back, her head bowed. But when she turned to welcome him home, he could see she'd been crying.

"Where were you?" she had asked. Only then had he noticed the time, how late he was.

"I had a patient come in with an infection. A man who had abdominal surgery last week. They had to operate again." He glanced at the clock above the stove. He thought again how late it really was. It was already past nine-thirty.

She turned back to the counter as he hung up his coat. And, this time, when he looked at her, the sniffing had turned into sobs and her shoulders were shaking. "I w-wanted d-dinner to be so g-good..."

"Jen. Baby." He remembered moving across the

kitchen to gather her into his arms. He remembered her lying her head against his shoulder. "Don't be mad at me. I should have called. I will next time."

"I—I'm—not m-mad at y-you…" she'd wailed. "I'm mad—at—that—s-stupid—stuff…" She'd pointed to a big pile of goo in the sink that looked like it had been spaghetti once. Now it was charred on one side and sticking straight up like quills on the other. "I'm—n-never—going to—cook—ever…."

To his credit, it was one of the times of his life he had done the right thing by her. She was only twenty-one and he knew how important it was to her to please him. He hadn't even cracked a smile. "I love you, whether you can cook or not. I love you, Jen…." He'd stood there for what seemed like forever just stroking her hair. Then, after he'd helped her throw the horrible stuff away, they'd ordered out for pizza, which they'd eaten picnic-style on the floor next to the fire.

What was it about today that made him remember the first few romantic months of their marriage? he wondered. Matches in hand he turned away from her, went back outside and started the grill.

Twenty minutes later they were munching away at the kitchen table.

"It's good," she said. "Better than good."

"I think so, too." He leaned back in his chair, stretching his arms up around the back of his head and crossing them there.

Her eyes met his. "Thanks."

He'd been married to this woman for six years. She'd always been pretty. But what he saw now was something more…something mature…and full and strong. Maybe, he wondered, he was just recognizing those qualities for the first time, seeing how she was devoting herself to Cody.

"So when are you going to use all those notes you took and start teaching me how to do therapy?"

"Anytime you want."

"As soon as we can," he said.

"That's fine with me."

One beat. Another.

"We should get back," she said finally, jumping up to begin gathering silverware and plates. "Cody'll be awake."

Michael stood quickly to help her. He stacked the glasses, then went to the sink beside her. They stood shoulder to shoulder. He set the glasses down. "Jen?"

"Yes." She turned toward him.

"Do you know," he whispered to her. "Sometimes I wonder what would have happened if we hadn't made so many mistakes with each other."

He heard her intake of breath, saw the emotion begin to pool in her eyes.

"Sometimes," she said, her voice as gentle and as smooth as her fingers would have been if they'd brushed against his skin. "I think about that, too."

Her hands were still in the sink, wet from the running

water, but he didn't care. He took them, suds and all, into his own and held them there.

When he pulled her to him, it was the first time in years, even when they'd been married, that she had felt so totally protected in his arms. He gripped her to him now as if he would never release her, ever. She could feel the solid pumping of his heart against hers.

She didn't pull away for the longest time. But she didn't turn her face up toward his, either. If only they could make this moment last forever. But they couldn't. They had hurt each other too much for that.

"Come on," he said to her as he let her go. "Guess I'd better get you back."

Buddy Draper sat in the front office of the Dallas Burn fidgeting like a little kid. He straightened his tie. He stretched his legs. He crossed his ankles. He wished he had worn a polo shirt and casual pants instead of this suit.

He was so far out of touch with the world of Major League Soccer that he hadn't even known what to wear when he came to visit Harv Siskell.

Harv Siskell. The man who had come to watch him play soccer at R. L. Turner High School his junior year and who had wooed him onto the team. Harv Siskell, who was too good a friend now to ever give up on him.

Buddy straightened his tie again, feeling more and more uncomfortable.

"Harv is ready for you," the secretary told him.

He practically jumped out of his chair and grabbed the packet of videos with both hands. "Thanks, Margaret."

She winked at him, which calmed him down just a bit. "It's good to see you back in this office, Buddy."

"Thanks, Margaret."

Harv stood beside the desk waiting for him when he entered. "Buddy. Come in. Have a seat." And then the man did a double take. "You look like you got dressed for somebody's funeral!"

"I couldn't decide what to wear."

"How about number fourteen?" He gestured toward one of Buddy's old jerseys hanging against the wall amid the many team photos and trophies. In big green numbers it said 14, with DRAPER above. After he had left the team, they had retired his number.

Both he and Harv stood looking at the jersey for a minute. "Brings back memories," Buddy said, feigning nonchalance.

"So." Harv took the videos from Buddy's hands. "You want to tell me what's been going on lately? How are things going with that beautiful woman in your life?"

Buddy shot him an astonished look. "What?"

"You know what I'm talking about. The pretty dark-haired lady you used to bring around to all the games before you forgot how to drive your car and crashed it."

Oh, Buddy knew, all right. "I don't see her anymore."

Harv sighed. "Sorry, kid. Guess she was just a

groupie, huh? Did she only want you when you were a famous Burn soccer player?"

Buddy thought about Harv's question for a long time. That hadn't been Andy's motivation at all. Andy wasn't like any other woman he'd ever known. "I wish," he said to Harv, smiling sadly. "It would have been easier that way."

"What do you mean?"

"Andy's a PT, she works with the kids at Children's Medical Center. When she heard I quit playing soccer, she let me have it. She didn't know that the front office pulled my contract. She thought I gave up because I wouldn't be the best anymore."

"Interesting." Harv took a swig from his water bottle. "Very interesting. And you never bothered to set her straight."

"She'd worked so hard to help me play again, Harv. It meant everything to her because she knew it meant everything to me. I couldn't tell her that all the hard work she put herself through for my sake just wasn't enough. All she could see was *me* giving up. And I'll tell you right now, Andy learned a long time ago not to let people give up."

Harv sighed. "She was a nice-looking girl."

"Still is."

"I'd sure like to see you moving ahead with your life instead of having to let so many things go."

"I'm going to be okay, Harv. I thought God had a

certain calling on my life, but he didn't. Or it changed. Or something."

"You could say it changed."

"I just have to find my new direction. The place God wants me to go next."

"Maybe I can help you do that," Harv said.

Buddy pointed to the packet of videos on Harv's desk. "Maybe you already have, Harv. It's been a long time since I've been this excited about anything."

"So? That mean you're interested in the job?"

"If I wasn't, I darn sure wouldn't have come all the way down here in this suit and tie."

"I want you to remember one thing while we discuss this," Harv told him, his eyes crinkled up in a smile. "I want you to know what you're getting into before you tell me you'll do it. Coaching from the sidelines is a lot different than being a player. Sometimes it's easier. Sometimes you see things a whole lot clearer. Other times it's more frustrating than you ever thought possible," Buddy said.

"I've had my share of that already," Buddy said.

He took out his notepad while Harv turned on the VCR and slipped in a game tape. Together, they spent the rest of the afternoon absorbed in watching the runners moving around the field.

Chapter Seven

Monday morning, almost two weeks after Cody had taken ill, Jennie returned to work for good. She had a million and one things to do; sketches to complete, staff to manage and an editor to assuage. But she could not stop thinking about Michael as she sat behind her desk with a thousand responsibilities weighing down on her.

Number one, I wanted Michael to hold me.

Number two, standing in that kitchen, in my ex-husband's arms, I didn't feel alone anymore.

And, number three.

Most important, this number three.

We had six years to make things work between us and we couldn't do it. What would be any different now? If Cody hadn't gotten sick, we never would have come back into each other's lives.

She absentmindedly shot a rubber band across the

room. It hit Art Sanderson on the shoulder as he passed by. "I hope that wasn't intended for me."

"I always intend them for you, Art." She aimed another one.

At that precise moment, Art disappeared into his office and the object of her previous thoughts stepped in, neatly dressed in an open-necked turquoise shirt that complemented his eyes and wavy blond hair. She froze, the rubber band still in hand. "Michael?" she whispered even though she didn't need to. "What are you doing here?"

"I've come to see if you want to hang out with me today," he said with breathtaking nonchalance.

"Hang out? Now?"

"Now is as good a time as any. Six Flags is open all afternoon."

"Six Flags?"

"I want to go somewhere with you, anywhere with you, that we can both relax and have a good time for a few hours. We deserve it."

She stood up and looked at him as if he were absolutely bananas.

"Is that so crazy? Is that so wrong? It's been so long and I...I just...." He walked over to her desk. "I needed to prove something to myself."

"Like what?"

"Like...what happened between us on Saturday wasn't just a figment of my imagination."

I'd give anything, she thought, *for someone to tell me what's right...what's wrong.*

Then, *I don't want to hurt over this man anymore.*

"Jennie."

"No."

"Please."

"No."

Suddenly he smiled. "It scares you, doesn't it?" he said very softly. "It scares you just as much as it scares me."

"What would I have to be scared about?" she asked. "I have no idea what you're talking about," she lied.

He went down on one knee. It was the most ridiculous thing she'd ever seen. "Go with me this afternoon. Please? I'll win you something. I'll get you the biggest, tackiest animal on the midway. I'll ride all your favorite rides twice."

"Michael," she reminded him. "This is my first day back at work. I'm swamped here."

"Is she giving you a hard time, Michael?" Art stepped out of his office.

"Well," said Michael, "apparently she's loaded down with work."

Art surveyed her desk. "Everything already waited a long time. There's nothing here that can't wait one more day. Just go, Jennie. Give yourself a break."

Art and Michael left her no choice. Michael brought the car around and they went on their way. They walked hand in hand among what seemed like hundreds of kids and teenagers. "What shall it be first?" he asked her as they stood watching the six flags of the different countries that had once claimed Texas for their own. The flags of France, Spain, Mexico, the independent Texas flag, the Confederate flag and the United States flag all snapped and rippled in the breeze.

She thought a minute. "The go-carts. I always liked the go-carts the best. Then the Log Flume and the Runaway Mine Train and the Spinnaker..."

When he stopped laughing at her enthusiasm, he had to ask her. "When's the last time you were here?"

She narrowed her eyebrows and thought back. "I must have been a senior in high school. We came here on a senior trip."

"We never came together, did we?"

"No. Remember? We were always going to bring Cody when he got old enough." But, when Cody had finally been big enough to ride all the rides, they'd been pursuing their divorce.

"I'm glad—" he said quietly "—we've found a spot on neutral ground."

"Neutral ground nothing," she said, suddenly smiling mischievously. "I'll take you on at the shooting gallery. Then you'll figure out we're not on neutral ground."

"Okay," he said, letting her take his hand and drag him. "You show me."

They rode rides all afternoon. She beat him three times at the shooting gallery. He teased her incessantly because one of the rides she wanted to ride wasn't there anymore.

"They've torn it down," he kept saying, "to make way for bigger and better things. That should make you feel old."

"Hush, you," she said, waggling a finger at him. "Today's been wonderful. It's made me feel young instead."

"But they've torn down the Flying Jenny!"

"It always was my favorite when I was a little girl," she admitted, honestly saddened.

"Probably—" he laughed "—just because it was named after *you.*"

"Leave me alone."

"Maybe I don't want to leave you alone."

They went to the Mexican section and he bought her a huge tissue-paper flower. They sat on a deck, watching twinkling lights flicker on all over the park, stuffing themselves full of enchiladas and refritos at El Chico's. After the waiter took their plates, he dared her to ride the enormous spinning Mexican hat they'd been watching across the way.

"After eating enchiladas?" she asked him, eyes huge. "You've got to be kidding me."

"Nope," he said. "I can handle it. Can you?"

"You're a doctor," she teased him back. "You shouldn't let people do this to themselves."

They paid for their dinner and giggled all the way to the giant sombrero. And, after it was over, they both wobbled off, panting and laughing, hand in hand.

"You look a little green," he commented.

"So do you."

He grabbed her hands again. "We'd better help each other along."

She said out of the blue, "We should have brought Cody here."

He looked at her sadly, remembering everything now that stood between them. "We should have." He changed the subject. "I promised to win you an animal, didn't I?"

"Yeah," she said. "Come to think of it, that's exactly what you promised me."

"Well, come on, then."

They walked to the midway, where he spent a fortune buying chances to throw balls at milk bottles and shoot darts at balloons and throw dimes in bowls. Finally he was victorious. The man behind the booth handed Jennie a fat plush pig with a flourish. "There you go, young lady."

Michael counted his change. "I think I just paid fifty bucks for that thing."

"Thank you, Michael." She shot him a little sideways grin that made her look sixteen years old. "I love him. I'm going to name him Petunia."

"Him? Petunia?" He threw his head back and

laughed. Really laughed. But she didn't laugh with him. Tears welled in her eyes instead.

"Do you know how badly I needed this?" she asked him.

He asked, "Are you okay, Jennie? Why are you crying?"

It was everything he could do to keep from bundling her against him again. But he wasn't going to do it here beside the ring-toss booth while she cried over Petunia the male pig. So he told her the truth. "I knew."

During their afternoon at Six Flags, they'd decided Jennie would start teaching Michael some of Cody's therapy the next day, at lunchtime. Michael parked the car, then stopped to admire one of the brightly colored paintings on the cement wall along the lot. Children staying at the hospital had done the paintings themselves, wonderful primary-color renditions of hopes and hurts.

How long, he wondered, *will it take Cody to be able to draw pictures again?*

As he boarded the elevator, Michael hated to admit he felt a little bit let down today. He'd been eager for some time to start learning Cody's therapy. But it was hard coming here after he and Jennie had gotten away yesterday. For a few hours he had forgotten all the challenges his son was facing. He felt guilty for forgetting. Guilty and afraid, because he'd held Jennie the other afternoon and he hadn't wanted to let her go.

The first person he saw when he walked into Cody's room was Jennie. Suddenly, he wasn't just scared anymore. He was terrified.

Their relationship had subtly changed over the past few days. He was attracted to her again.

Father, I never intended to feel anything for her again. It didn't matter. After Cody got well, Jennie would go back to drawing cartoons and ignoring anything that didn't advance her career. He'd go back to long hours with his practice and the hospital, taking duty calls at all hours of the night. Despite what had happened to Cody, he and Jennie were still the same people who'd divorced each other. Nothing would ever change that.

At the sight of her, he remembered the day four years ago, when they had faced each other in the courtroom. Jennie had sat quietly, tears and anger in her eyes.

"Your honor," his lawyer had said. "The grounds for this divorce are irreconcilable differences. Both Michael Stratton and Jennie Stratton have informed the court that the marriage cannot continue. There is no fault involved here, although Michael Stratton is the party who actually filed in court."

"Does Jennie Stratton agree with that statement?" the judge had asked.

Her lawyer looked at Jennie. Michael looked at Jennie. She hesitated ever so slightly, then nodded.

"Yes, your honor," her lawyer had said.

And so, their marriage had ended. Michael's heart

had flooded with relief and guilt and grief. Once upon a time, maybe they had loved each other. Or maybe, they had only thought so.

"Hi, Jennie," he said quietly now as she turned toward the sound in the doorway. "Hello there, little guy." He took Cody's hand and focused all his attention on his son.

Andy Kendall arrived, looking brisk and cheerful. "Therapy time," she sang out. When she saw both of them standing together, she smiled at her little patient in the big hospital bed. "Ah. Today my student is a teacher. So I just get to sit and watch." She sat down in the plastic chair and propped her feet up playfully. "Go for it, Jennie."

"You have to critique," Jennie told her. "I want you to watch me and tell me everything I'm doing wrong."

Andy inclined her head with a knowing smile. "Oh, I will."

Jennie laid her notes on the bed and surveyed a page before she started. Then she began to demonstrate shyly to Michael as she spoke. "This is how you do it. As you sit and talk to him, at least three times a day, you need to work his leg muscles like this."

Michael watched her for a while, then she stepped back so he could try it. It was almost funny, being so formal with each other today. Michael moved Cody's leg up and back, up and back, with one hand pressed firmly against the ball of his foot, the other gently bent around his knee.

"You're doin' it, Dad," Cody said. "You're doing it just right."

"You sure are." Andy nodded, too.

"That *is* just right," Jennie told him. "Perfect."

"Aw," Michael said, not quite so afraid anymore. "Of course it's perfect. I wouldn't have it for Cody any other way."

"Now," Jennie instructed him. "Next we do this…and this…and this…" The lesson went on for over half an hour, while the two of them worked side by side. By the end of the session, Andy had left, giving them her approval, and Jennie was blowing streams of iridescent bubbles through a tiny blue wand.

"Get 'em, kid, let's get 'em," Michael egged Cody on, relaxed now and totally engrossed in the movements as he and Cody tried to pop as many bubbles as they could as they wafted up over Cody's head.

Cody was giggling then, finally, laughing, a great belly laugh as the room filled with bubbles. And just as Michael was deciding that this therapy session was almost as much fun as the day before at Six Flags, one of the biggest bubbles landed right on Jennie's head and sat there.

"Mom's got a bubble on her head," Cody cried. "Look, Dad. Mom's got a bubble sitting right on top of her."

"Get it off," Jennie said, not moving.

She raised a hand to brush it off but Michael stopped her. "No. Don't. It's a *sign.*" He made a pass over her head with his hands. "Stand there and see how long it'll stay."

"Michael, I don't want to stand here all day with a bubble on my head!"

All three of them just looked at each other. Cody snorted first, and pretty soon they were all laughing so hard their stomachs hurt. Jennie's bubble had long since been exploded into oblivion. And still they laughed.

It had been ages and ages since they'd laughed together like this. And following on the heels of the incredible despair Michael had been feeling only days ago, it felt like a miracle.

He reached across Cody's legs and gripped Jennie's hand. How he hoped that she felt the miracle, too.

"Come on, Cody," Jennie said. "Let's try sitting up again. Can you support yourself with this arm?"

"Yeah."

"Watch this." She showed Michael how to prop Cody's arm against the pillow like a tent pole. "There you go. Let's see how long you can do this. Michael, time him."

Michael crooked his arm up so he could read the watch on his wrist.

I remember it now, Jennie thought. *I remember why I fell in love with him. He cares so much about everything.*

And I remember why I fell out of love with him. Because he cared more about everything else than he cared about me.

At that precise moment, Cody started to wobble.

Jennie grabbed an arm to stop him from falling.

Michael grabbed an arm to stop him from falling.

Which meant they all grabbed each other. And then, even though their middles were still aching from the last onslaught, the three of them started laughing all over again.

Mark Kendall stood in the doorway to Andy's apartment, hands in pockets, legs crossed, leaning jauntily against the jamb. He looked like a kid ready to play a practical joke on somebody. But this felt much, much better than a joke.

"Had to stop by," he told Andy, straight-faced, when she opened the door. "I've got something for you."

"What is it?"

He pulled the white legal-length envelope from his jacket and handed it to her. Andy ripped it open impatiently, tearing the paper in little accordion-folded chunks. She pulled the two tickets out and stared at them in puzzlement.

Mark didn't say anything. He just stood there, waiting for her to figure it out.

"Burn tickets? For tonight's game?"

"Yeah." Mark shrugged. "Just thought it was something you might want to be in on."

Andy hated to dampen Mark's spirits, but she hadn't attended a game since Buddy Draper had retired. She didn't think she wanted to do it now. "What would I want to be in on?"

"You should be thanking me, you know," he said

instead of answering her question. "This game sold out two weeks ago. I had to work miracles to get tickets, especially after the paper came out with Harv Siskell's announcement."

"What announcement? What did Harv Siskell say?"

"Ah," Mark said, grinning.

"Well?" She couldn't help it. She almost shouted, he had her so frustrated. "What's going on?"

"Perhaps you should take a look at today's paper. Or maybe you should Google the Burn to see what's going on."

Andy rushed off to find the paper. Returning with it to the living room, she scattered it in sections across the sofa. "What exactly is it that I'm supposed to read?"

"Try the sports section," Mark suggested. "Page eight."

She counted through the section with her thumb then opened the page, shaking it once to dispense with the wrinkles.

"You see it?"

She scanned the page. "Just a minute…let me…"

Then she saw the headline.

Draper rejoins team, it read. *Former player to coach Burn beside Harv Siskell.*

"Buddy's back" the story began. And, really, that was all she needed to know. She stared at the dark newsprint, unable to read because her vision was blurring.

"So," Andy said, still leaning against the jamb. "Maybe the guy listened to you after all."

"Buddy had a hard time listening to anybody."

"You never know—" Mark pointed out "—what an impact you might have made on somebody's life."

Andy threw the newspaper at her brother, trying to cover the conflicting emotions churning within her. *Especially to me. Especially to a God who wanted to take charge of Buddy's life.*

Mark fended off the paper with both hands. The sport section fluttered to the floor. "So what do you say?" he asked.

"I say he'll make a great coach. Coaches are good at bossing people around and not listening to a thing anybody tells them."

"Hey," Mark said, grinning. "I take exception to that. I'm a coach, too, remember?"

"Oh. Sorry. Forgot that," she said, eyes wide, feigning innocence.

"No, you didn't." As he spoke, he fashioned page eight into a giant airplane and sailed it back at her.

She sobered for a moment, looking down at the airplane by her feet. "I guess I should read the rest of the story."

"Doesn't matter. I'll tell you on the way to the game. How do you feel about all this, Andy?"

"I don't know," she said honestly, knowing she could never sort out everything inside her heart just now. "I'm glad for him. And sorry it took this long in coming. I feel like he lost so much."

"I'd say late is better than never. Tonight's his first night back on the field. I knew you'd want to be there."

"Buddy! Buddy!" the lady shrieked from behind him. "Good to have you back, Buddy!"

He turned and acknowledged her with a nod, then waved at another fan higher in the stands who was holding up a banner that read: WELCOME BACK, BUDDY.

Harv, standing with arms crossed, leaned sideways and said, "See? I told you, didn't I? They haven't forgotten you. They won't for a long time."

"Tell me this isn't a marketing ploy by the front office, Siskell," he growled. He was already perturbed by the carefully orchestrated press releases that hit the stands this morning. "Tell me you really want me standing beside you telling these poor players what to do."

"Hey," Harv said. "We brought you back, and the Galaxy brought back Beckham. I'd say front offices all over this league are working at marketing ploys. *But*," Harv said, grinning, "I really want you standing beside me telling these poor players what to do."

Buddy stared straight ahead. The Comets' left forward kicked the ball toward the Burn's goal. Miraculously, the keeper blocked and deflected the ball to the right side.

Buddy crossed his arms just like Harv and concentrated on the game. He still had a lot to learn. But though he didn't say anything to Harv, standing on the field with the huge lights above was everything he needed, whether the fans remembered him or not. The tart, earthy scent of the stadium, of fast food, of the players. The sharp surreal sounds of the whistle blowing and the crowd cheering and the glare of the lights. The players grunting with exertion and the smack of leather or leg against the spinning ball.

Thank you so much, Father, he thought, *for showing me my own pride. Thank you so much for bringing me back here.*

Chuck Kirkland, left forward, trapped the ball and crossed it to the left side. Marshall Townsend, striker, passed the ball back to the defender, who passed it to the right forward.

"That's a clear shot," Harv shouted, jerking his arms to his sides. "Take it, Spooner! *Take it.*"

Spooner trapped the ball and shot it back toward Townsend. Marshall took the shot. The Comets' keeper blocked it with his fist, smacking the ball off to the left side.

Harv pounded his fist against his open palm to accentuate each word. "No. No. No! Spooner, what were you thinking? Townsend couldn't make that shot!"

Buddy commented offhandedly. "If he'd made it, you'd have been slapping him on the back and taking both those guys out for a New York strip dinner."

Harv growled. "I would have let him have a piece of my mind. For a chance at stardom, he turned down a sure thing. The only player I've ever had who could make those shots was you."

The halftime discussion was peppered with Harv's colorful phrases and a handful of diagrams on a dry-erase board on the sidelines. Buddy stood rigidly by his boss's side, feeling that he had nothing to contribute. A few minutes into the discussion, he turned his head sideways a bit and, for one moment, he thought he saw a vision. He saw her climbing up the steps in the stands not far from him, wearing a bright red dress, carrying a bag of popcorn. "Andy..." But she wouldn't be here, not after the way he'd treated her, not after everything that had gone between them.

But there had been a time when she believed in me more than I believed in myself. There had been a time when she believed in God more than he did, and maybe that had helped her see things he couldn't.

Buddy straightened his back, shifted his gum to the other side of his mouth, and turned to the players. Harv had already moved down the line after finishing with Townsend. The team was just starting back on to the field. "Hey, man," Buddy hollered at Townsend, a teammate he'd played beside not so very long ago. "I only have one thing to add to that chewing out you just got from Siskell."

"Well," Townsend tensed, he was waiting for Buddy to heap the criticism on, too.

"If you try a shot like that next time—" Buddy shouted, smiling "—just be sure you're going to make it."

Chapter Eight

The next morning, as Jennie lay in bed halfway between sleep and wakefulness, the telephone rang. "It's me," Michael said without preamble. "Cody's doctors just called. Can you meet us at the hospital some time today."

Her heart skipped a beat. "What is it? Is he sick again? What's wrong?"

"He's fine, Jen. But his doctors have written an evaluation on him. They're presenting the results and they want us there."

"What time?"

"They'd like us there about nine-thirty."

"I'll see you then." She threw back the covers and started in on another day caring for her son.

When she arrived at the hospital, Michael was waiting for her in the lobby. "Am I late?"

"No," he said. "Just on time."

They stood there, looking at one another.

"We probably should sit down," he said, breaking the silence between them. Yesterday, the silence had been comfortable. The laughter had been so spontaneous. Today, it was not.

They sat as though frozen, within hands' reach but not touching, barely breathing.

The seconds ticked by, until Andy entered the room and motioned for them to follow her. As they walked toward the doctors' conference room, Michael didn't take Jennie's hand the way he had yesterday and the day before. The easy rapport between them was gone.

Michael had wondered if Cody would be at the meeting. He was glad now that he would not be. This wasn't the place for a child, certainly not one whose dreams hung in the balance of what the doctors might tell them.

The interns filed in one by one. Jennie glanced at Michael, wondering if he could still see himself in these somber young people who stood waiting to declare a verdict on their child. One of them handed Michael a manila folder that contained the typed report.

"This outlines Cody's progress and will tell you what we expect from him during the next months," the intern began. "We will go over it with you verbally now. Tonight you can go over it together and contact us if you have questions."

So cold. So clinical. A little boy's limbs…their little boy's life…

"We can't promise you anything," the intern continued.

"Well," Michael said impatiently. "Tell us what you can. Please."

"We believe Cody's muscle control may come back over time, especially in his arms."

"And…"

"His legs may be more difficult to bring back."

"Which means?" Michael took a step toward them, daring them to tell him the worst.

"We believe Cody will *not* be able to walk again."

"What?"

"We don't believe that your son will be able to walk in the future."

"No." It was too much for Jennie. "Don't say that."

She took one step forward and Michael grabbed her arm. "Nobody knows, Jennie. You mustn't lose heart. They have to give us their opinion, but it might not mean anything. Not really."

And because it's part of the profession the intern continued. "We recommend surgery on the left leg. The muscle tightness there could pop your son's hip out of joint. We'd recommend severing that muscle before it causes a problem."

"No," Jennie whispered. She turned tear-filled eyes toward Michael.

"But you've got to know that while severing the

muscle will solve the problem with the bone, the resulting damage to the muscle will leave it permanently weak."

Michael turned back to the interns, knowing from the sudden slump of Jennie's shoulders that he had to get her out of the room fast. "Thank you." He tucked the folder under his arm and steered her toward the door. "We'll go over this. Then we'll get back to you."

He didn't let go of her elbow. They walked out side by side, their heads held high, past the row of interns and doctors who thought they knew Cody's fate.

How could you have ever been so pompous, Michael thought. *How could I have ever been so sure that I knew someone's fate?*

"You want to go in and see Cody?" he asked her.

Jennie shook her head. She couldn't bear that right now. "No. I can't."

"Come on, Jennie. Let's go for a walk." He wanted to take her outside into the beaming sunshine and into the fresh air, any place that might bring them peace after the news they'd just received. But he knew they wouldn't find peace anywhere. *Oh Father,* he prayed. *Help us.* As they started toward the stairwell, they passed the small gymnasium where Andy conducted her sessions.

"Simon says," Andy's voice rang out, "put your finger on your nose."

Five children, all happy and sitting in line in wheelchairs, touched their noses.

"Good," she said. "Very good. Now. Simon says wiggle your right hand."

Five right hands wiggled.

"Now, wiggle your left hand."

One left hand wiggled.

Jennie halted in the doorway, riveted to the scene. Michael gripped her forearms and hung on to her. He wanted to be her life preserver. "Michael." She looked up at him like someone drowning. "Please. Take me somewhere. Get me out of here."

"Come on."

He wrapped an arm around her waist, propelling her to safety. They raced down the steps and burst through the polished glass doors.

She took her first desperate, labored breaths of fresh air while Michael held her up.

"How can they say that?" she said, her voice raspy with pain. "How can they stand there and say that to our faces and expect us to accept that he won't walk again?"

He gripped her shoulders. "They had to do it, Jennie. They're doctors. They have to assess the situation as they see it."

"Who gave them the right to pronounce that sort of sentence on his legs? Who gave them the right to tell us what Cody can or can't do? *Who gave them the right?*"

"Jennie." He held her at arm's length. "Stop and think

about it. *We* did. We gave them the right. We wanted to know what they had to say."

She looked into his eyes, his dear gentle eyes that had calmed her during so many storms, that had been as cold as death once, looking at her from across a courtroom. Today, in the blaring sun, they held every bit as much pain in their sea green depths as they had held then. Pain. And frustration. And anger.

Anger. She stopped short, realizing it for the first time.

"You aren't accepting what they're selling, either."

"I'm not accepting it."

"Why?" And, in the moment she asked it, she saw him flinch. She could answer the question for herself. She could see it in his expression, too. "You've done the same thing to someone."

He struggled to make her understand. "It's a judgment call. It's one of the most difficult things a doctor has to do."

For the first time, she saw what he had been up against all along in his work, and their marriage. She hadn't known that he'd had to make these kinds of calls when he'd left her every day. That realization came as another blow. *He failed me in our marriage. But maybe I failed him, too. How much of a buffer could I have been for him then?*

He hugged her around the shoulders as she went to him, nestling against him as he held her there. Despite her sorrow or, perhaps, because of it, she clung to him without reservation now, without restraint. And the emotion that soared within her made her feel as if she were balancing on the edge of a dangerous precipice.

Here was the attractive fair-haired boy she'd fallen in love with once.

Here was the grown man she'd grown disillusioned with and disappointed in.

Here was the man she wanted to kiss her more than she'd wanted anything in her life.

He hadn't shaved this morning and the prickles of hair left dark contours around a jaw that had once been less severe, not so firmly set and a mouth much more prone to widen into a smile. His eyes, the true green color of the grass after spring rains, spoke volumes. They told her what she instinctively had already known. He wanted a kiss just as much as she.

He whispered her name. "Jennie."

When she felt him holding his breath, it was as if time had stopped, as well. Ten years ago...six years ago... four...

He bent toward her. His touch, not as soft as it once had been but grittier now, was more demanding. He purposefully moved toward her mouth, and she turned slightly, knowing how well their lips fit together.

For a moment she was nineteen again and he was twenty-one and it was the first time they'd touched each other. He held her so close she could scarcely breathe.

Neither of them was the same as they'd once been. They were tied together by a painful past, and by their love for the little boy who lay in the bed on a floor above them.

His hands went to her shoulders and he held her slightly away. When he did, she saw the empty indentation on his finger where his wedding ring once had been.

She saw a broken marriage and years of pain.

She saw the nights Michael hadn't come home and the ways she'd accused him of abandoning her.

She saw all the ways they had failed each other.

"Michael?" she asked reluctantly. "What are we going to do about the surgery?"

He broke their gaze for a moment. He stared up at the clouds drifting by above them. "We're going to let them do it."

"No," she said, shaking her head and looking determined. "We can't."

"What do you mean 'no'? You heard what they said. The surgeon recommended it."

"She *recommended* it. Dr. Phillips didn't say it was something we had to do."

"Believe me, Jennie. The woman knows what she's talking about."

"But you said yourself it was a judgment call."

"An educated judgment call. Jennie, we'll have a meeting with her and discuss it. But I already know what she's going to say. The orthopedic surgeon here has a wonderful reputation. She's trained for years to deal with situations like this one."

But Jennie wasn't giving up. "I was in Cody's room when the surgeon examined him. She came Tuesday morning at seven-thirty. Andy hadn't even had a chance to come in and work with Cody's legs yet. He was stiffer than I've ever seen him. The doctor didn't see him at his best."

"Fine, then. We'll get a second opinion. Is that what you're telling me you want?"

"I'm telling you that even if we get a second opinion, I won't be able to agree to let them damage a perfectly healthy muscle."

"Jennie, the doctors wouldn't suggest it if they didn't think it was the best thing for him."

"Twenty minutes ago you told me there is always hope. Now you tell me there isn't any."

For the first time, Michael's impatience was evident in his voice. "That isn't what I'm telling you at all. If Cody's hip comes out of the socket, he could be in pain for the rest of his life."

"But what if it doesn't happen?" she insisted. "What if we ruined Cody's leg muscle for nothing?" Why, just once, couldn't they agree on something as important as their son?

"You'll have your way no matter what happens. We have joint custody. They won't agree to surgery without both of us consenting."

"The surgery would make it so much harder for him to keep moving forward. Everything in me says we should avoid surgery at all costs."

"And everything I know," Michael told her stiffly, "leads me to believe we should follow a doctor's guidance."

She stood before him, nose to nose, bristling with defensiveness. "Because you're a doctor, too," she said.

"Yes."

"You may be a doctor. But you're also human," she stated. "Humans make mistakes."

"Yes. You seem to always need to remind me of that." He stared at her angrily, his eyebrows in a tightly knit curl, his face as hard as granite. "You aren't going to let me forget that, Jennie, are you?"

"Not—" she said quietly "—as long as my son's future hangs in the balance."

Chapter Nine

Cody couldn't have asked the question at a worse time. He looked right up at both of them that afternoon, his eyes wide and full of hope, and asked, "Do you *like* each other again?"

Michael stared down at his son, covering his pain with a blank expression.

Jennie stared, too. "Honey…" she said after a long, awkward silence.

"Cody…" Michael said just a half beat later.

"I *said,* 'Do you and Mom *like* each other again?'"

"Why would you ask a thing like that?"

"Because you're being funny around each other. You look at each other and then you don't look at each other."

Michael glared across the bed at Jennie. He'd look at her all right. He'd look at her with all the blame he could muster in his eyes.

Jennie glared back.

Lord, Michael prayed. *Help us know what to say to him.*

Jennie's pinched expression softened somewhat as she touched Cody's hand and sat on his bed. "Darling."

Michael knew she spoke slowly because she was searching for words, trying to be as honest as she could with him. "Your dad and I will always care about each other, mostly because we share *you*."

She glanced at Michael and then down again.

At that exact moment, Michael and Jennie faced everything they needed to face. It was time to stand before Cody and answer the questions they'd been asking themselves each time they'd been drawn to each other these past few days.

The answer came swiftly. "The together part of our lives is over, Cody," Michael told his son with an air of finality, steeling himself not to look at Jennie. At last, at last, she would know for certain where she stood with him. "Your mom and I tried to be married once and we couldn't be. That's how we have to leave it."

The little boy's eyes, eyes that had been sparkling with happiness only moments ago, began to fill with tears. "But—y-you come here t-together all the t-time and laugh and I thought—I thought…"

"We're here together because of you, Cody," Jennie told him in no uncertain terms.

His little face twisted with pain. "But I don't like you being d-divorced all—the time. I want us to live in the same h-house. I want us to live in the same p-place. I get—mad having to move around all the time—and none of my friends know where I—a-am—when they want to come p-p-play."

"They know where you are," Michael said, but even in his own ears the words sounded insincere.

"They know you live at my house on some days and at your mom's house on others. Lots of kids do that."

Cody's voice rose to a wail. "B-but—I d-don't w-w-want t-t-tooooo."

Jennie tried to gather him into her arms but he wouldn't go.

"I w-w-want…to…b-b-be in our old h-h-house when we were all together," he sobbed.

Michael stood above them, feeling more helpless, if it could be possible, than he'd felt when Cody had first gotten sick.

Tears slid down his cheeks, as if he'd been waiting for this minute to express his full grief. "Please like each other again and then me and Mason can stay in the same p-p-place…"

A nurse stuck her head in the door. "Is everything okay in here?"

"No." Jennie's voice stayed firm as she held Cody's little head on her knees. "He's getting really upset."

Michael and Jennie sized each other up. Michael could feel everything built between them during the past few days, every faint hope, every vague possibility, shattering into bits.

"I'll go," Michael said. "I don't know what else to do."

"I'll stay with him," Jennie said as Cody wept into the lap of her denim skirt. "I think you *should* go."

Michael shrugged into his coat and bent down to Cody.

"I'm going to head out for a little while now, okay?"

But Cody wouldn't turn to him. So he left, casting one backwards glance at the two of them, Cody and Jennie, two blond heads bent together on the bed.

Father, it seems like everything I touch, I ruin. It seems like everything I try to heal, I destroy. Silently, he shut the door and headed for his empty home.

That night, just after eight o'clock, Jennie pounded on his door. Neither spoke until he had hung up her coat and ushered her into the den. There each took up a position facing the other and squared off like prize fighters, each sorting through a welter of feelings and having no idea what to do about them.

"I didn't know what to say to him!" He slammed his fist on the fireplace mantel. "'Yes, son. I've been kissing your mom in the parking lot. What do you think about that?'"

"Well, you couldn't be honest with him. After all—" she said tersely, repeating his words from only hours ago "—it didn't mean anything anyway."

"Of course it didn't."

"They had to call an intern and sedate him."

"Why didn't we see this coming? We were idiots. *Why* didn't we see it?"

"There were a great many things we didn't see coming, Michael."

He looked at his ex-wife. He didn't dare voice all the things he was sorry for. *For Cody being so intuitive. For the way he himself questioned God. For letting his guard down. For needing Jennie.*

"It was a perfectly natural assumption for Cody to make," she said quietly. "We have been there for him. We've been there *together.*"

"I know that. We've misled him."

"Have we?"

He looked directly into Jennie's eyes. And, because he was aching inside and feeling cornered, he didn't think to soften his reply. "I would not fall in love with you again, Jennie. My life has changed since you and I were together."

"You're talking about your newfound faith?" She gave a harsh laugh. "You have all the answers now, don't you? You got me to pray, but those prayers didn't help at all."

Michael ignored her jab. "And we mustn't forget your career…"

"My career was never more important than *you.* I *waited…*"

"I'm not talking about me. I'm talking about what happened with Buzz Stephens."

"Oh." Her spine went as straight as a stalk of Texas grain sorghum. "You're going back to that, are you? You never did understand how important that cartoon was to me. It was one of my first really *big* successes."

"Buzz was one of the nicest guys and the best doctors I'd known. Because of that cartoon, the IRS delved into his finances. He lost his practice because of your big *success*."

"He did it to himself," she reminded him.

"And you had to make certain everyone knew that," he said.

"I've had enough," she said as she advanced on him. "Did you hear me? I said I've had *enough*. I hate private practices. I hate internships. I hate med school. I hated waiting up for you all night long. I hated being in love with you and thinking I'd grow *old* and we'd never get to spend time together. You weren't even there to drive me to the hospital when I went into labor with *Cody*..."

"I met you there," he threw back angrily.

"After you'd finished delivering someone else's baby. I think that's the loneliest I've ever been in my life, lying in that birthing room waiting for you."

"I know I did that to you," he said bluntly. "I would probably do it again. I'm a doctor. And sometimes that doesn't leave me with choices."

"All I ever wanted..." She started to say it but then let the words trail off. It was just too personal to her now and too painful. *All I ever wanted,* she wanted to say, *was to know that I was important to you, that there were times you might have wanted to choose me.*

"I'm *glad* Cody forced this issue," she said. "I'm *glad* he asked that question out loud so I could hear your answer. I'm not going to make the mistake of thinking anything might be different between us no matter how different you say you are. And I'm not going to let *any of this* hurt Cody."

"So help me God, I do not want Cody to have any more disappointments. He's had enough already. And heaven knows what is still to come." They still hadn't told Cody about the interns' assessment of his legs. Or about the surgery they couldn't decide on.

Her eyes asked the question. What are we going to do? "I thought we were doing it the right way...." His hands came to his face now and covered his mouth. He inhaled through his fingers and closed his eyes. "I don't think he ought to see us together again."

"I know that, Michael." And when she agreed, the irony of it shook him. They had *started* this, begun to draw together, for Cody's sake. And it had hurt him instead.

They stood there for the longest time, while the minutes ticked between them.

Jennie shoved her hands into her pockets, doing her best to seem nonchalant, trying to pretend that pulling away from Michael wasn't hurting her. She turned away to look out the big window overlooking the backyard.

As Michael stood watching her, seeing everything she was trying to hide, he berated himself for past mistakes. *Father, I really wasn't there to drive her to the hospital, was I?* How many times had he deserted her without being able to see?

I take you, Jennie, he'd vowed, to have and to hold, from this day forward."

To have and to hold.

"We have to schedule our visits so we aren't at the hospital at the same time," she said.

He nodded, never speaking.

"He's reading too much into our being together."

"I know that."

"And we're reading too much into it, too."

"Yes." They were toying with something that would have been devastating to each other. They didn't dare risk it again.

Father, help me know what to say.

"I've needed someone during all this, Jen. Someone who understood how much I loved Cody." *And I had no right to want you to be the one...because there were so many times when you needed me and I wasn't there for you.*

"We've shared our lives..." She trailed off again.

"No," he said. "Not really. We shared a bed. I don't know that we ever shared our lives."

She looked at him solemnly, as if she had just lost something very important. "You're right. We didn't."

She picked her purse up and tucked it under one arm.

He stood and held the door for her. There was nothing left for either of them to say.

"Goodbye, Michael," she said as she stood close.

"Goodbye, Jennie," he said.

She was wearing the winter white wool coat she'd arrived in, her gold hair fanning out in ribbons around her shoulders. He'd never seen her look so lost as she did standing on his porch beneath the floodlight.

Chapter Ten

Andy Kendall sat with Michael and Jennie the next day, face-to-face, and told them exactly how much Cody's emotional outburst had cost him. "It's a physical setback for him," she said. "He's exhausted today. Our staff has decided it would be best to let him rest. We'll start his therapy again in several days…when he's ready."

Michael slumped against the wall, his arms crossed, his head bowed, trying not to appear as defeated as he felt. "You tell us what you think would be best, Andy." How he was beginning to hate these diplomatic words. What would be best…give it a try…read the assessment.

"I have something else to discuss with you," Andy added. "Something that might not be as easy to accept."

"We want to do everything we can," Jennie said, her hands together in her lap.

"Tell us," Michael agreed.

"I've had a long discussion with the child-life psychologist here at the hospital. We both agree that you need to begin thinking about Cody and his home life when he leaves the hospital. His world will need to be kept very, very stable."

"He has a stable home," Michael said too quickly. "In fact, he has two of them."

"That's exactly what I'm talking about," Andy answered. "The psychologist and I think the two of you need to decide to keep Cody in one home for a while. At least until he's stronger. We both believe it would be for the best."

For the best. That phrase again.

Michael felt as if every bit of his power was being stripped away. And somehow, even though the woman sitting beside him had no more control over the situation than he did, he felt as if Jennie was winning a round. What Andy was suggesting undermined their joint custody agreement.

"This is what you think he needs?" he asked, feeling trapped. "How do you know what's best for him? We've given him everything we know to give him."

Father, please, don't add this, too.

Jennie, too, could not remain silent. "We've tried to be careful," she said. "We've tried to set things up so we could all three live with them." She had known all those years ago that they couldn't make this decision alone.

It had taken the lawyers months to come up with the original joint custody arrangement.

"We wanted Cody to have *everything*," Michael said, his voice gravelly with emotion.

And yet, Michael reminded himself, *Cody never had everything he needed since the divorce. He never had both of us.*

Each time Jennie stopped in to see Cody, Cody talked about Michael.

"Dad came to see me last night," he said from his pillow. Jennie always suspected he was studying her face to see her reaction.

"That's nice."

"He had a talk with Mason."

"Oh?"

"He said he'd come to see Mason again this afternoon about two."

"I'm glad." She had to be back at the *Times-Sentinel* then. "How are you feeling today?"

A toothy grin this time. "Fine. Andy's been telling me about the swim team again. She says I'm getting closer."

"Great. That's my Bear!" She tousled his hair. "I can't wait. I promise you right now I'll buy you a new bathing suit."

"Yeech." He made a face. "Do I have to go to the store and try it on?"

"No." She laughed at him. He was a lot like Michael,

he hated shopping for anything. "I wouldn't dare put you through that torture."

"Good."

She started on his therapy and worked with him until after one forty-five, desperate to make a difference in his leg muscles. Michael was due back any minute and she had to get back to the paper. "See you later, darling." She bent and kissed him. "Have a good visit with Dad."

This time, when Jennie left him, she felt the same as all the times before. She felt as if she hadn't done nearly enough for her son.

"Did you see that request from the *San Antonio Sun?*" Art Sanderson asked her when she got back to the office. "They want to run some of your statewide stuff."

"I saw the request."

"We may consider putting you into syndication," he said casually. "I'll bet we could get several of the biggest dailies in Texas to pick you up. It would be a step up in your career, Jennie. And a coup for the *Times-Sentinel* because we have you."

"It looked interesting."

"You don't sound as excited as I thought you'd be."

"My mind's just been on other things, Art."

The phone rang on her desk. She picked it up. "Stratton here."

"Jennie? Andy Kendall from the hospital is on line three."

When was her heart going to stop pounding every time a call came from the hospital? "Thanks." She heard the line switch and she immediately pounced on Andy. "What is it? What's wrong?"

"Nothing's wrong," Andy said. "I needed to talk to you and I didn't have a chance today at the hospital. I don't want to discuss these things in front of Cody."

"What things? What is it?" Then, she heard herself. "Oh, Andy. I'm so sorry. I'm just at the office and I—"

"It's okay," Andy said. "I didn't mean to scare you. I just need to bring you up to speed. One more of these 'you may not agree with me but I have to tell you anyway' things."

Jennie steeled herself with a deep breath. "Let's have it."

"The orthopedic surgeon examined Cody again today. His left leg is worse. If we're going to fight against the surgery, Cody needs more therapy time. I discussed it with Michael, too. I can only give him so much. I have other patients to work with, too."

Jennie's heart stopped for a moment. "What did Michael say?"

"He's willing to devote more time if you are. But he probably doesn't see the urgency of this matter the way you do. He told me he thinks surgery is the best answer."

"I know that." She stared at the scattered piles of memos and letters and cartoons on her desk. She stared at the full calendar that hung on the wall beside her phone. All she could think of, as she stared at it, was that things on this calendar did not go away. When she pushed them back, just as she'd been doing these past weeks, they piled up and up on top of each other until they threatened to make the entire twelve months fall off the wall.

How could she do more than she was already doing? "Maybe if I came in at night. That way I could spend another two hours with him." She already gave him therapy for an hour each morning and another one every day after lunch. Art had been wonderful to help her work it into her schedule. "But Cody's always tired then." The logistics of it all were staggering. Add to that an eight-hour workday that sometimes spilled over into a ten-hour one. And, despite her crazy schedule, she was lonelier than she'd ever been in her life.

She laughed, a tired little chuckle that betrayed how defeated she felt. "Maybe if I gave up sleeping, I'd have time to do everything I need to do."

"We've got to come up with some workable answer. I'll try to get in to work with him a third time this evening. I don't want him to lose what he's gained. I thought he was doing so well."

"Andy." Jennie sat down in her desk chair. "Thank you. For everything. I know how hard you're trying, too."

After Jennie hung up the phone, she stared at it. *Who am I?* she asked herself while she sat glaring at the receiver, thinking of Cody lying in the bed needing her. "How much further can I stretch myself?" she asked aloud.

"What's that?" Art asked, walking toward her. "Do you remember the meeting in my office? We've been waiting for you for ten minutes in there."

"Oh, Art. I forgot!" She jumped from her desk, banging the drawer with her knees, and went flying into his office. But as she sat and listened to everyone's comments, all she could think of was Cody. Staff members talked about problems they were having and things that had changed and cartoon opportunities the paper had missed while she had been gone. She somberly authorized Art to send some of her work on to the *San Antonio Sun*.

After the meeting closed, Art cornered her. "Jennie? Is there a way you can rearrange your schedule to be here at noon tomorrow? I've got a photographer setting up to do some group shots of the staff. I thought we'd do some of you alone, too, and send them on to the *Sun*. That works for everyone else."

"I can't do it, Art. I can't be here at noon. That's when I give Cody his therapy."

"You can't change it? You can't do it another time?"

"No. I already go once in the morning." She was on the defensive now and she hated it. She felt guilty about it all, but she could only stretch so far. "I can't go after two because Michael—" She stopped. She couldn't explain it. It was just too complicated for anyone else to understand.

"I wish you could work this out for me," Art said.

"I do, too. But I can't."

In the end, Jennie took her frustrations out on a piece of pen-and-ink paper, shading in a cartoon she'd already designed. She didn't like it when she finished. She started all over again.

BELOVED, CALL ON ME.

It didn't matter that she never had time to sit down and read a book or write to a friend. She didn't care that she didn't have time to putter in the garden or run or go out to lunch with friends. All she cared about was Cody.

I SENT MY SON TO DIE THAT YOU MIGHT LIVE.

She didn't know for certain whether Michael's words made everything seem clearer today...or if today gave her new perspective on his words.

I had forgotten about what happened with Buzz Stephens, how that hurt Michael.

She did not hear the voice prompting her to open her own heart. Instead, she heard her own questions. *Have I done that?* she asked herself. *Have I closed people out, did I close Michael out, because I was afraid to make myself vulnerable to him again? And did I use the* Times-Sentinel *to do it?*

She didn't have any answers. She only knew she owed it to herself to ask. *I'm losing control of everything else and Cody's going downhill, too. Cody needs me. More of me. All of me.*

She buried her face in her hands and scrubbed her palms against her scalp, frighteningly close to tears. She didn't know what choice she would have made four, five, even ten years ago. But she knew what she would choose today.

Three minutes later, she stood in front of Art's office, trying to appear casual. "You got a minute, Art? We need to talk."

He held the door open for her then. He leaned back in his creaky chair with a slight frown. "What is it?"

"I'd like a leave of absence, Art. I need time away from this."

"No. You can't do that right now. Not with this offer of syndication from the Texas dailies. Take my word for it. This is not the time to disappear."

"There's never a good time to disappear."

"We could go national in a year. I'm talking Washington, D.C. You could be the Anna Quindlen of cartoons."

She knew how much she stood to lose. At any other time in her life, Art's words and talk of "might be's" would have tormented her. But not today...not now...not with Michael's words still echoing inside her head. "I know all those things, Art." Suddenly, she felt very, very tired and afraid. This decision was something totally new to her. She would never have considered it before.

Art took a breath and gave her his most genial smile. "Maybe we don't have to decide this today, Jennie. Take the time to think about it. Give yourself some breathing room. You're putting pressure on yourself when you don't have to."

"I'm not putting pressure on myself."

"You're doing this because of what's happened to Cody?"

"Yes."

"You've got other options. Consider those. Hire a private nurse."

"A nurse isn't the same thing as a mom. Right now Cody needs a mom." And, to her surprise, the more she argued for it, the more she knew in her heart of hearts that this was the right choice. "Perhaps someday I can come back to this. But it's not as important as my little boy."

"I think you're making an emotional decision at a very bad time, Jennie."

"Cody needs me. He needs me beside him at the hospital. When he gets out, he needs me driving him back and forth to outpatient care. He needs me to do therapy about five times a day." And Andy was still talking to her about getting him onto Mark's swim team but they hadn't set a date for that yet.

"Do yourself a favor. Sleep on this. Don't do anything drastic."

"It isn't drastic, Art. It's just a leave of absence. It's something I have to do."

"It's bad timing."

She gathered all her strength. "If you'll give me a

leave of absence, I'll take it, Art. If you won't, I'll resign. This is *that* important to me."

"You can't do that. Jennie, your *career.*"

"It's going to be tough," she said with a little smile. She could tell by his expression he was going to give in to her. "Cody and I'll have to learn how to live on a lot less money." A *lot* less. But it could be done. She would just have to stop serving microwave dinners and bake some real food like chicken and potatoes and meat loaf. And she was certain Michael would help her if things got too bad. "It's worth trying, Art."

He smiled sadly. "I can see you think so."

Before, this would have been the very moment she gave in to her own self-doubts. Now she knew how much was at stake for her and for her son. "I do."

"Okay," Art said. "I'll give you three months."

"Six months."

"You're kidding."

"I've never been more serious in my life. I can't *afford* to kid about this. I'm working at keeping my priorities straight."

"Don't say I didn't try to talk you out of this. Go clean out your desk."

In forty-five minutes, her desk was bare. Her spirits were heavy even though she knew she'd done the right thing. She loaded her car full of cardboard boxes of awards and portfolios and framed letters and was on her way…to a new life…a new place…where her son was waiting for her.

* * *

The first place she stopped to relay her news was the child-life center on the bottom floor of Children's Medical Center."

She couldn't wait to tell Cody. "Hey, kiddo!" she greeted him. "I've just done something *wonderful*. I quit my job for a while so you and I can hang out together!"

He beamed at her, eyes enormous.

"I thought we'd play checkers on the bed and tell more stories and have more therapy," she told him. "What do you think?"

"I think you're the best."

She squeezed him tight and reveled in the boy smell of him. "That's exactly what I was hoping you'd think."

Andy swept out of the next room, clipboard in hand. "Hi, Jennie."

"What time does Cody need his next therapy session? I'm here to do it. And I'll be here tomorrow. And the next day. And the next and the next and the next."

Andy had started to turn a page on the clipboard but she froze. "What have you done?"

"Took a leave of absence. Told them if they wouldn't let me have a leave of absence I'd just quit."

"No way."

"I did. I blew my editor's mind."

During the days that Jennie came to give Cody his therapy, she and Andy began to be friends. Andy told

Jennie about her years growing up with Mark and how Mark had decided to start the swim team. Jennie told Andy about her time at university and how she met Michael.

Andy asked her one afternoon, "Are you doing anything after Cody's therapy? I've got to get a present for my brother. Maybe we can have a quick lunch, talk about something besides therapy and interns and surgery for a while."

Jennie laughed, a happy sound that let Andy know what a weight had been lifted from her shoulders during the past weeks.

"I'd love to. It's been about a year since I've gone shopping with a friend."

Later that afternoon, they strolled through the Galleria, watching the ice skaters spin on flashing blades, two friends now, two women on common ground.

Andy led them to a little shop filled with sports logos on rugs and underwear and dog collars and even Christmas ornaments. "Is your brother a football fan?" Jennie asked.

"No," Andy said, leading her to one specific corner. "A soccer fan." Everything on the shelves here was red and blue, emblazoned with the words: Dallas Burn.

"Look at these." Jennie pointed to a collection of beer steins imprinted with the team's logo. "Those are beautiful. Cody had played soccer every summer. Has Mark always liked the Burn?"

"No," Andy said, her voice quiet again, enough for Jennie to notice it. "He had occasion to meet somebody on the team. After that, he really became a fanatic."

"Who? Who did he meet?"

It was still so hard for her to say his name. "Buddy Draper."

"*The* Buddy Draper? Boy, he was great! I'm not a big soccer fan myself but I loved watching him play. That was too bad about the car accident he had."

"Yes," Andy agreed tonelessly as she moved away up the next aisle. "It was." She found a "Parking for Burn Fans Only" sign and started toward the register. "I'll get this. He'll think it's great."

Jennie followed her. "Didn't Buddy get hurt badly in the accident? He never played again after that, did he?"

"No. And no." Andy fumbled in her purse for her wallet. "He never played again. And he didn't get hurt badly in the accident. He got hurt just badly enough that he couldn't be the *best* anymore."

"Is that what you heard?"

"Yes. Sort of."

"What do you mean, sort of?"

Andy didn't answer. She focused all her attention on signing her sales receipt, and handing it to the clerk.

Jennie asked about Buddy Draper again as they crossed the parking lot. And so, Andy told her. "That's why *I* think he stopped playing. Jennie, he told me he wanted to play soccer more than anything. Then, one day, he decided he didn't want that anymore."

Something in her tone must have told Jennie there was more. "Why would a famous soccer player come to Children's Medical Center for therapy?"

"Because he already knew me."

"From before?"

"From long before." And then Andy decided to finally tell Jennie the rest of it. "We were seeing each other for a while."

They climbed into the car and slammed the doors. "Oh," Jennie said, looking embarrassed. "I had to ask."

"Yeah. You did."

Jennie shook her head. "Maybe you're lucky you never got any further than that. Look where marriage got me." But she had memories of Michael she would always treasure. And she had Cody, too.

Then Andy said, "Can I ask a nosy question?"

"You can ask it. I might not answer it."

"You and Dr. Stratton? Did you ever think about trying things again?"

The hesitation wasn't even perceptible. "No."

"You're both doing so much for Cody." Andy locked the car. "And it seems like there could still be something between you."

"It's been a battle every step of the way," Jennie said with decisiveness.

"Can I ask you something else?"

"What?"

"What happened in your marriage? What made things go wrong between you?"

It was Jennie's turn to sigh. "What happened between Michael and me was very, very subtle," she finally said. "When we took our wedding vows, it's as if we vowed to be in each other's lives but not in each other's hearts. We were so young. We thought a career and money and a rewarding lifestyle were supposed to come easy. A *relationship* was supposed to come easy. But it's not like that. It really never was, you know?"

Andy nodded. "Thinking back to it, I just got disappointed in Buddy. I have to watch these kids trying so hard for every little victory. Buddy is so talented and I felt like he wasn't trying at all. I went through this time when I couldn't understand him anymore."

"Michael worked thirty-six-hour shifts during his internship at Parkland. I was supposed to be this happy newlywed, welcoming him home with open arms. I never saw him except when he was exhausted and strung out and too drained to give any attention to what we had. So I turned around and channelled all my frustration into my work. I worked the same horrible shifts he did, only I did come home for a few hours to sleep, which he couldn't do. Then, when I got pregnant with Cody, I thought things would be different. I thought the baby would make us both different. But it didn't. It just got harder."

"Didn't you ever talk about it?"

"Sometimes. But not soon enough, Andy. Not soon enough. I wasn't there when he graduated med school. He wasn't there when I went into labor with Cody. It's like we just quietly needed each other without crying out. And then, one day, there was just too much pain between us…so much pain…something we could never overcome. And we blamed each other for it."

"End of story."

"End of story."

"But you are both there for Cody now," Andy said softly.

"That's how things happen when you have kids together," Jennie said. "No matter what goes on between the two of you, the thing that holds you together is your children."

Chapter Eleven

"Bill," Michael told his patient as they sat together in the consultation room, Michael's white coat unbuttoned over his shirt and tie. "Your blood pressure's sky high again. Have you been taking your pills?"

"Did for a while, Doc," Bill Josephs told him smugly. "Then I decided they weren't doing me a lick of good. Didn't make me feel better at all. In fact, I started feeling a lot better after I quit those things."

Michael shook his head and wagged a finger at Bill. "You are the most stubborn patient I've got. If I didn't like you so much, I'd pawn you off on some other physician."

"Well, why take medicine if it doesn't make you feel good?"

"Those pills *do* take some of your energy away, Bill. For your heart's sake, you've got to keep your blood pressure down. Have you been resting?"

Bill nodded. "Yep. Taking a nap like I'm four years old again but I'm doing it because you told me I had to."

"Good. Are you walking?"

"Nope. I've been riding one of my horses. And I've been fishing a lot. Figured that would make up the difference. You should see the seventeen-pound carp I caught the other day. Biggest sucker to come out of Lake Sam Rayburn in a long time!"

"Have you been drinking decaffeinated coffee?"

"Don't ask me about the coffee."

Michael laid his chart down on his lap. What exactly could he write in his records about Bill Josephs after *this* checkup? "You haven't been obeying my orders."

"Of course I've been drinking coffee. Had to have something to jump-start me after those pills you gave me. They made me feel like Marge's old Aunt Enid."

"Is she a relative in Dallas?"

"No, sir." Michael saw Bill's eyes sparkling and he knew the man was about to crack another joke. "She died back in 1957," Bill said, chuckling. "That's why I don't want to feel like her."

Shaking his head, Michael wrote out another prescription and handed it to his stubborn patient. "I should call Marge in here and tell her how difficult you're being."

"Don't do that," Bill said. "I won't ever hear the end of it."

"I know that, which is why I'm giving you a reprieve. This is a different prescription. These pills aren't quite so potent. And—" he leveled his eyes on Bill's "—if *these* don't work, call me and we'll find something that does."

Bill raised his eyebrows. "Thanks, Doc. I'd just as soon not get Marge involved in all this. I love that old woman but she's stubborn. Won't let me do things my own way."

"I know that. That's what I like about her," Michael said, laughing. "I know she'll make you follow my instructions."

"We'll see you next month." Bill donned an old tweed hat on his head. "Don't send me a bill. I'll pay out front."

Once Bill Josephs had left, Michael had plenty of other patients to take care of. "Shelby Landon's charts are on your desk, Dr. Stratton," his nurse told him. "We need you to sign release papers on your desk," his receptionist told him. "There's a salesman who wants to talk to you about a new arthritis drug," his nurse said.

"Thanks, Inez. Will you get the MMR ready for room four."

"Sure."

"Thanks."

Michael went to his office, picked up the little girl's charts and thumbed through them. Clipboard in hand, he opened the door to room four and faced a young mother with a toddler in her arms. "Hi," he said smiling. He had delivered Shelby sixteen months ago. He took the little girl in his arms. "I can't believe she's grown so much." He held Shelby out from him so he could look her straight in the eyes. "Shelby," he told her, "you're going to be in college before we know it."

"Oh, no," her mother said, laughing. "Don't rush her. She's just learning to talk!"

He sat on his stool with Shelby in his lap. "Okay," he kidded. "One thing at a time. We'll let you learn to speak first. We'll deal with the valedictorian speech later." He handed Mrs. Landon a pink page of instructions to care for her daughter after this latest inoculation, and outlined the side effects.

"Expect her to run a low-grade fever. We'll give her a dose of acetaminophen while she's here. In about ten days, she could *possibly* have a light case of the measles."

Inez came in to administer the injection and Michael showed Mrs. Landon how to hold Shelby in her lap with the girl's little leg securely tucked between her own. Shelby took the shot like every other child. She waited a moment, let the pain sink in and started to wail.

Michael held her again when Inez was finished. "She'll be fine," he said to the mother. "It won't hurt but for a minute."

As if on cue, Shelby stopped crying. She grabbed his glasses and started to chew on them.

I do care about my patients, he thought. *But I don't care about them as much as I care about my family.* But it niggled at him now, the words Jennie had said. Because he couldn't be sure he'd always felt that way. If he was brutally honest with himself, he'd admit there were times he'd gone for days working and not thinking of Jen.

When Michael arrived at the hospital, he told Cody about all of his patients, including Bill, and they laughed together. But for some reason, the laughter wasn't as much fun without Jennie around.

"Did you know you were gonna be a doctor when you were little? When you were my age?" Cody asked him as they sat watching TV.

"Mmm." Michael thought for a minute before he answered. "You know what? I guess I did." He gave one short little chuckle, remembering. "I shouldn't tell you this but I used to bring all kinds of animals home when I was a boy. I always tried to doctor them and make them better. I brought home frogs, a mouse and a turtle. I did okay until your grandmother found a dead snake under the bed."

Cody leaned forward intrigued, the television forgotten. "Did it die under there? Did you want to make it better?"

Michael shook his head, remembering the boyish seriousness with which he had approached his task. "I was about your age, Cody. It was dead when I found it. I didn't understand some things then. I thought if I treated it I could bring it back to life."

"You were crazy, Dad!" Cody said, laughing.

"It's one of the hardest things a doctor has to face,

you know? That you can't bring anything back once it's been taken away." He gripped his son's hand, feeling sudden emotion rising within him. It was the first time he thought to be grateful, truly grateful to God, that his son was alive.

He said, "Only God can make new life come out of something that's died. The way he did with Jesus." *The way he did with my heart.*

They squeezed hands. Cody said, "I know that."

Michael said, "I'm so thankful to God that your mother and I still have you."

And Cody had gone back to the previous story again. "So what did Grandma do when she found the snake under your bed?"

"She hollered at me."

"Why? You were just trying to help it."

"Think of what your mom would do if she found a dead snake on the carpet."

"Mom would kill me."

"Your mom would kill *me*," Michael said, laughing. "She knows this story from way back. She'd know you were taking after me." He surveyed his son seriously, his heart filled with pride and sorrow. "You think you want to be a doctor when you grow up?"

"No. I don't want to be gone from home all the time like you are."

His answer might as well have been a kick in the stomach. Michael looked away, trying to compose himself.

Father, was I gone so much that it even mattered to Cody? Of course. Of course I was. So Jennie wasn't the only one it mattered to.

He turned back to his son. "So what do you want to be when you grow up?"

"A professional snowboarder."

"Oh. Good."

"Or a professional biker like Lance Armstrong."

"Right."

"Or maybe—"

"I think you'd better stop," Michael told him. "You'll give me nightmares."

"Or maybe I'll just be a professional bull-rider. Like the ones we saw when you took me to the stock show in Fort Worth."

"Cody…"

"Just kidding, Dad," Cody said, grinning and his eyes smiling, too. He struggled to hold his arms out to Michael. "Love you, Dad."

When Jennie stepped outside the elevator toward Cody's room, she heard Michael's deep, booming voice from all the way down the hallway. "She hollered at me."

"Why? You were just trying to help it."

And so the conversation went.

She didn't intend to eavesdrop. She just didn't have anywhere else to go. So she stood outside, listening to them laughing, feeling cut off from them, until the door opened and Michael stepped out. Closing the door quietly behind him, he leaned against the wall and wiped his eyes with the back of one sleeve.

It didn't occur to Jennie to be embarrassed or to slip away. She stood silently watching him until he realized she was there. He rocked forward on his feet, his hands in his pockets, and turned toward her.

She gave a little shrug. "I was just about to go in to see him."

He jangled his keys in his pocket and looked angry, as if he thought she'd been spying on him.

"You don't have to be mad. And you don't have to hide what you're feeling. The last thing I want to do is make you feel like you have to conceal yourself around me." She paused. "Believe me, this is hard for me, too."

Michael rode one thumb back over his shoulder, pointing toward the room where Cody lay. "*He's* the bravest one of all."

"No, he isn't," she said quietly. "He just doesn't know to be afraid."

Michael stared at the ceiling. "I want him to get better. I want him to grow stronger."

"So do I."

They stood for a moment looking at one another, each of them thinking it had been a long time since their wants had been so entirely focused on the same thing. "Did you know I took a leave of absence from my job?" Jennie said.

His eyes shot to hers. "You did?"

She nodded.

Michael stared at her in disbelief. "What did you say to Art?"

"That my son was more important—" she looked at him pointedly "—than anything else in the world to me."

"That was it? That was all there was to it?"

"That was it. I cleaned my desk and left." She shrugged her shoulders, half disbelieving it herself. "I didn't even give them an hour's notice. I just took off. And that may have been the easy part. I'll have to learn how to get by on my savings for a while. I'll miss the money."

"I'll help you. You know that." In their divorce settlement, he'd agreed to pay alimony if she ever had to stop working. He hadn't begrudged her that at all. But he couldn't believe she'd really done it. Until now, the *Times-Sentinel* had meant everything to her. "Jennie." He didn't have to say anything more. He knew she understood how much he admired her.

"I know. It's amazing, isn't it? I told him if he didn't give me a six-month leave, I'd just quit. And he *gave* it to me. Just like that." She snapped her fingers.

"But your job, Jen? It was so important to you."

"Cody needs more therapy."

"You know I'm helping with that."

"He needs more attention than ever now...especially if we're going to avoid the surgery."

"That's what you're thinking of? Avoiding the surgery?"

"It's what I'm always thinking of now."

"I see." Into his mind came the doubts once more. Had Jennie left her job to support Cody, or had she done it so she might win her way?

"I can always go back to the *Times-Sentinel*. I haven't burned any bridges." But she didn't really know how long Cody was going to need her. Maybe six months. Maybe forever. She sighed. "I got to thinking you were right. I shouldn't have let my work become so all-important. Maybe I should have given Cody a higher priority a long time ago."

"No." Michael reassured her. "You were usually there for him. I wasn't." Cody had just told him as much.

And Michael wondered, *Am I living my Christianity with the same blindness that I used to run my life?*

Cody, of all people, made him begin to question that.

Chapter Twelve

"Hi, Cody." His best friend, Taylor Cowan, stood at the foot of his bed. "We miss you at school. I came over so I could bring you some stuff."

Cody leaned forward in his bed, a gesture as unaffected as if he'd just woken up from a sleepover. "What did you bring me?"

Taylor emptied his pockets and came up with a roll of cherry Life Savers, a Tony Romo football card and a roll of quarters for the arcade games at the hospital lounge—and a letter from his teacher, Mrs. Bounds.

"Dear Cody," the letter said. "We're thinking about you every day and hope you get better soon. Taylor promised to deliver this letter to you. Can we bring the class and visit soon? Are they taking good care of you there? Would you like me to put together a packet of studies for you? (You'd better not say no!) In geography, we're learning about Africa. We're reading about a troop of baboons that lives in the desert of Namibia. They can survive without water by eating berries and figs. It has been an interesting study and I think you're going to like it. See you soon! Love, Mrs. Bounds." Right behind the letter was a piece of green construction paper, signed by everybody in his class, that said Get Well Soon.

"My mom says you can come over to our house and spend the night as soon as you get out of here." Taylor plopped on the side of the bed.

"I can't walk around very much," Cody told him, testing him.

"That's okay. We can still hang out and play Madden."

"I'll ask Mom. Or Dad." Cody frowned slightly. "I don't know where I'll be. I'll probably be at Mom's on Fridays."

Taylor pointed at the stuffed animal on a shelf beside the bed. "You still sleep with that?"

"Nope," Cody lied. "Not on your life."

Just then, Andy came in. "Well, hello," she said to both boys.

Cody made one sweeping motion with his arm that thrilled Andy. Two weeks ago, he hadn't been able to move his arms nearly as well. "This is Taylor, he brought me this stuff."

"Looks like you're having a good time." She grinned at Taylor. "You want to stay while Cody has his therapy?"

"Yeah, sure." Taylor stood on tiptoe, leaning over, his small freckled nose propped right on top of the chair where he'd been sitting.

Andy began working with Cody's left leg.

"How come you're giving me therapy now?" Cody asked. "I thought we always just did this in the morning."

"The head orthopedist is coming to check you out in a little while. I found out an hour ago that she's got you on her schedule tonight." As Andy worked, she asked the boys more questions, not wanting Cody to sense how very important this doctor's examination might be. "So, does Taylor live close to you?"

"He lives close to my mom. I'm going to spend the night with him when I get out of the hospital."

"Do you guys really sleep when you spend the night or do you keep the Playstation burning all night long?"

Taylor grinned. "It's Playstation 2, Madden 2007."

Andy cuffed Cody on the shoulder. "That's what I figured."

An hour later, the orthopedic surgeon arrived to examine Cody, flexing Cody's toes and rotating his leg while Jennie and Michael watched from opposite sides of the room. Andy had called them both when she'd seen Dr. Phillips's schedule.

"Don't know," the surgeon said as she splayed the bones of Cody's foot apart with gentle pressure. She watched closely as he flattened the limb against the heel

of her hand. The examination lasted a few more min-
utes. When it was done, Dr. Phillips asked Michael,
Jennie and Andy to accompany her to an empty lounge.
Turning toward them, she glanced at Jennie, then her
eyes leveled on Michael's. "I have to tell you, I still think
surgery is the best option for your son." Michael heard
Jennie take a ragged breath. "I think it would be best.
But it's fair to tell you that there's room here for doubt."

Michael felt his annoyance growing. He'd always
hated that phrase. Room for doubt. *Father, why can't you
give her wisdom, give her a clear picture? Why can't you
give me a clear picture so we can just move forward?*

Andy said, in a fit of inspiration, "Cody is as limber
as he can get. If you can't make an assessment this way,
I'd suggest a series of X rays. We'll know how the bones
are angling if we do it that way."

And for the first time in a long time, Michael felt like
a prayer he'd uttered might actually have been answered.

"Hmm." Dr. Phillips nodded at Andy. "That's not a
bad suggestion." Then, "Is the patient up to doing X rays
tonight?"

"I don't see any reason why not."

"I'll order them then."

Andy included both Jennie and Michael when she
spoke, "I'll go in to the X-ray room with him. I can keep
him limber, and I can help hold him in position. I can
make sure these pictures turn out the best that they can."

Once everyone left the room, Michael paced like a

caged cat. He stood gazing out the window for a moment, then brought his fist down on the radiator so hard he'd have a bruise for a week.

All he could see right now was the woman directly across the room from him, standing ramrod straight, her shoulders at a slight angle to him. It seemed as if the disagreement over Cody's surgery represented everything in the world that stood between them. And, in a way, it did.

She must have felt his eyes on her. She looked up, caught his glance, then turned away again.

"She couldn't tell us *anything*." He gestured his frustration into the air. "Not one thing."

"The X rays might help," she said to the window.

"Why is this happening?" he asked mostly to himself, the frustration feeling familiar now, like something he could hide behind. "Why all this helplessness?"

Jennie had her fingers on the window latch; she stared at her own hand as if she stared at something far away. "You never were the helpless one." When she spoke, there was a gentleness in her voice that he couldn't read. "You always knew what to do."

He let out a deep, shuddering sigh. "You know I only want the best for him, don't you?"

She smiled sadly, wearily, looking once more into Michael's eyes. "Michael. Of all the times I've questioned you, I've never questioned how much you love your son."

"All these years as a doctor, and I've never known how the patients feel at times like this."

"It's quite the discovery, isn't it?" And he wasn't sure he liked the touch of irony when she said it.

He had to say it. "You could agree with me, for once. About Cody's treatment. That would make it so much easier for us."

But she was shaking her head. "No, Michael. Not about something as important as this."

A pause. "You never were willing to compromise."

She wheeled on him again. "Is this the point where you remind me of all my bad character traits?"

"That isn't what I'm doing."

"Let's make a promise to each other. Let's agree not to remind each other of our failures." There had been so many of them, the nights he hadn't come home and had been unavailable to her emotionally, the times she had left the house on the edge of squalor because she'd been overwhelmed and depressed trying to work and manage a baby, too. There had been the times she'd met him at the door with a list of instructions, the hot water heater needed his attention tonight! The credit card company called and it was his fault they'd gone over the limit.

But Michael's exhaustion made him push it. He couldn't stop himself.

"I'm telling you," he blurted out, "that it took eight years and a deadly disease for you to finally realize what your priorities are."

"Michael! Think about me! This all began because I needed something to fill my hours the way the hospital filled yours! Don't you think I look at that little boy in there and know I made a mistake when I let the paper take over my life? At first all I wanted was to be there for you, Michael." She said it again as if to make certain he'd heard her. "It was *all* I wanted."

"Then where were *you* when I needed you, Jennie?"

"I said *at first.*" Her voice dripped with condemnation.

Her controlled stoicism only made him angrier. "Did you *once* stop to consider that I had no other choices then? Did you once stop to consider that we might not have any choice now?"

She backed up against the wall, eyes half closed, looking utterly drained, almost ready to slide down to the floor. "No."

"You've got to *accept* what Cody's facing. And, when you do, then we have to discuss *real,* practical solutions. Do you think I—"

"I liked you better—" she interrupted him "—when you were raging because you're helpless."

The door swung open and here came the nurse pushing Cody's wheelchair. Andy followed close behind them.

Michael and Jennie both waylaid her at once.

"What did she say?" Jennie asked.

"When will we know something?" Michael asked.

There were parts of Andy's job that she loved and parts that she didn't. There were times when a family asked her something spiritual and she was finally free to answer. Other times, she was forced to hold her tongue because she worked in a secular hospital. She wanted to say to them the way she'd said so many times to Buddy, *It's bigger than we are. There's someone else you need to talk to about this.*

"The doctor has surgery first thing tomorrow morning, and she won't have time to look at these until her office hours are over tomorrow."

"It's still going to be over twenty-four hours before we *know* anything?" Michael felt ready to hit something with his fist again.

"At least."

"She didn't say anything at *all?*" Jennie asked. "She didn't give you any indication which way she was leaning?"

"Not about the surgery." Even though Jennie had become her friend, Andy couldn't help but feel accosted about it at the same time. But then she brightened. "Dr. Phillips *did* say one thing."

They both asked about it at the same time.

"She spoke with the interns on Cody's case. No matter what she decides to recommend about the surgery, she agrees it is time to release Cody. It's time for Cody to go home." And she turned to visit another patient, her footsteps brisk along the corridor.

Home. *Home?* And which home might that be? Michael and Jennie stared at each other in the parking lot.

Something new and dangerous to sort out. They'd been too preoccupied with Cody's surgery to consider this yet.

"We'll have to decide, won't we?" Jennie asked.

Exhausted, they stood staring at each other. "There are times—" Michael pulled the keys from his pocket "—when I wish I could just give up...when I could let my defenses down...but I can't."

"There's no end to it."

A tree-lined curb lined the lot where Michael had parked his car. She sat down wearily on it. Michael sat beside her.

"I'm selfish and I know it." She studied the grass as if it were the most intriguing thing she'd ever seen. "I can't give him up, Michael. I want him *home* with *me*."

"I can't do it, either. Jennie, I fought for him harder than I've fought for anything. He's my life, Jen. He's the only thing I've got. You know that."

She nodded.

"We're moving forward, I guess." She gave him the slightest glance and a wry smile. "If we can't agree, at least we can be honest with each other."

"Yeah," he said. His voice sounded cracked. He cleared his throat and tried again. "Yeah." Clearer this time, his voice still soft, but low and disconcerting.

Just as she was about to stand, Michael reached out and caught her elbow. She gasped in surprise and turned her head slightly away.

"Jennie?"

She hesitated before answering. "What?"

"I wouldn't put you through this," he told her softly. "I'd stop hurting you if I could."

"It seems there's no end to that, either."

"It should have been over a long time ago." His thumb was rough on her bare arm and she shivered.

"Perhaps…" She didn't lift her face, yet he knew she could feel him watching her. "Someday it will.

"Michael, I've got an idea." She would never have suggested this, would never have even considered it, except for the things Michael had said about stopping the hurt. "What if Cody still changed houses but we gave him longer in each place? What if he spends two weeks with me, then two weeks with you? Then we could go back to the other schedule when he's stronger."

"Two weeks with you? Two weeks with you first?"

"I didn't say that. I was just giving an example. Or if we got another house and Cody stayed where he was, and we switched places?"

"Maybe. It might be an answer."

"All your talk about trusting God," she pushed. "Sometimes I wish that you would just trust me."

And neither of them realized that, as they talked of this someday ending, the answer they sought would bind them together instead.

"Andrea Kendall had been right to suggest the X rays," Dr. Phillips told Jennie and Michael the following evening. "I liked what I saw. Cody has at least a thirty percent range of motion, which is borderline. It doesn't mean surgery is out of the question…say in the next three months or so. But, for right now, I have to say we'd be better off to take a wait-and-see approach."

Jennie's heart soared. She was too happy right now to even think of saying I told you so. Three more months. Three more blessed months. If she and Cody worked hard enough until then, the unthinkable might never happen.

The news stunned Michael. He stood watching his son and his ex-wife as if he couldn't believe what he had heard.

"I told you, Mom," Cody said, his tousled blond hair sticking straight up from his cowlick like the crown on a rooster. "I told you I'd show Dr. Phillips a thing or two. See. Here's one." He pointed to one leg. Then he pointed to the other. "And here's two."

Michael left the room before Jennie. But five minutes later, after Jennie had kissed Cody goodnight, she found Michael still waiting for her.

"Hey." He was leaning against the wall just outside the door. "I don't know why you're not rubbing this in."

"Rubbing it in?"

"All this time, I've been trying to convince you to do the wrong thing."

She realized that, in his indirect way, he was apologizing to her. "Michael." She was desperate to make him understand. "No matter what you seem to think this isn't a competition about who's right and who's wrong."

"We'll have to deal with it again," he reminded her. And it won't be a competition then, either.

"If I've learned anything through this—" Jennie spread her hands wide, palms up "—it's to take things as they come. I'm going to work my butt off and I'll worry about that part of it when it gets here."

"What did Andy say?" he asked.

"Three days. He'll be leaving the hospital in three days. I'm going to hire a lady to do some of the housework. That way I can spend extra time with Cody on his therapy."

"I've hired a nurse to stay in the house with him and do his therapy with him while I'm gone."

"Michael…" So it was coming to this again. "Let him be with me first. I'm going to be *home*."

When he heard her words, his face twisted. "Jennie, I can't. You know that. I want him, too." The thought that came plunged him into despair. *Father, because of what happened to Cody, she doesn't trust me anymore. It happened on my watch.*

The physical attraction was easy.

Trust wasn't.

"Jennie," he said. "Can't you let go some? I'm not going to let what he's gained so far slip away. And I'm not going to let him slip away from you."

"I've got him signed up for swim class. I can start taking him next week."

"So can I."

"You mean the person you *hired* can start taking him next week."

Really that wasn't the issue and they both knew it. With all the custody possibilities they'd discussed, it came down to this. Jennie didn't trust him with Cody anymore. And Michael wasn't so certain he trusted himself, either.

"Michael," she said, reading his heart in a way she'd never been able to do before, "I trust you with him, if that's what you're thinking."

"I'm not." His voice was suddenly fierce. "Why would I be thinking that?"

"It could have happened when I had him, too."

And so she *had* thought of it, he knew it now, how Cody had been with him when everything started going wrong.

With a heaviness that threatened to topple him, Michael rummaged in his pocket and pulled out a quarter. "Cody's the important one. Not us."

"He is. The last thing we ought to do is put him through more conflict."

"Then are you willing to try it this way?"

"You want to *flip* a quarter for him?" she asked, aghast.

"I want everything to be perfectly fair for both of us."

"Nothing has been fair for us, Michael. One of us will win. One of us will lose."

"It's the only way I can think of." And, suddenly, for Michael, that seemed very, very important. She recognized that he wanted to be completely equitable for both their sakes. They both could picture Cody's face. When they'd told him that their marriage hadn't worked, that they wanted to live in separate houses. They both could remember the anguish on his little face, the question, no matter how young he was, that this might somehow be his fault.

She waved one small hand in the air. "Do it then." She hugged herself, squeezing hard, as if she had to hold herself in. "This will decide it." She made a vow to stick by the result of the coin toss, no matter what the outcome.

"You call it, Jennie."

"I will."

Michael held out his hand, closed his eyes and sent the coin flying.

"Heads." The quarter flew through the air. It hit the tile floor, bounced twice, rolled across the terrazzo. It spun around three times in smaller and smaller circles. Then, it fell.

They walked over to it together, each of them peering to see what it was, before he bent to pick it up.

Jennie said it aloud first. "Tails." Her voice broke. "He goes with you."

"Tails." Michael, torn between joy at his good fortune and sympathy for his ex-wife. "Jen…"

"You said so yourself." She shrugged but he knew she was devastated. "It was an unbiased way to decide.

"You and I," she stated simply, "have always been out for ourselves. Since the beginning and maybe even before that. It's about time we just *stopped*."

Michael had no reply. "I know how much this must hurt," he said.

"You don't know what's inside me, Michael. You never did. You never tried to know."

He closed his eyes at the sting of her words. "If I had tried, Jennie, you wouldn't have let me."

She looked up at him, her face still as a statue, her features so stiff they might as well have been etched in marble. "What does it matter now, anyway?"

Michael didn't see Jennie again until three days later, when she came to the hospital on the morning of their son's discharge.

"Well, Bear," she said as cheerily as if she were sending Cody off to camp. "Be good for your dad. Make sure he takes you to swimming on Tuesday. Andy's brother will be there. It'll be fun. If you need something and your dad's not around, call me. Sound good?"

"Yeah."

She rumpled his spikes of hair so close to the color of her own. "Love you."

"I love you, too, Mom."

"Your dad's going to bring you to group therapy with Andy these next two weeks. Be sure and work hard."

"I will."

"Where's Mason? Do you have Mason?"

"He's in the suitcase. Dad packed him."

"This kid weighs a ton," Michael said as he stood with

Cody draped across his arms. "Clear the way so I can set him in the car." He gave her a reassuring smile, trying to say with his expression what she would never accept in words. *I know this is hard for you. I'm glad you came.*

When she tried to laugh, it sounded too happy, forced and brittle, like something that might break. "You two had better get out of here."

He hoisted Cody higher. They were halfway to the BMW before Michael heard Jennie running behind them.

"Wait!" she called out breathlessly. He turned to see her trailing a bag from F.A.O. Schwartz in one hand. "I forgot! I've got things for him."

Michael reached his car. He tried to fit his key in the lock but couldn't while he held Cody.

"Here...Michael." She had her composure back as she caught up with them. "Wait. Let me get the door, okay? Here." She took the keys from his hand and quickly unlocked it.

"Thanks, Jen."

He bent in and settled Cody on the passenger side.

"I forgot all this stuff," she said, still panting slightly. "Presents." She handed them in to Cody, then backed away. "You can open them when you get to your dad's, Cody. I know you two are in a hurry now."

Michael leaned back against the fender of his car and crossed his arms. "We aren't in that big of a hurry. Now that I've gotten him into a seat, I mean. Let him open them here."

No words of agreement came from Cody. They both looked to see him already ripping open the first box. "A new swimsuit!" the little boy cried. He held it up to show Michael the suit with pirate insignia across the seat.

"Ahoy, maties!" Michael said, feigning a pirate accent. "Ye better be watching out. There'll be a new captain sailin' the seas!"

Cody held up the next surprise from her, a huge poster of the Dallas Cowboys.

"For your wall. At your dad's house."

Next came Guitar Hero for Playstation 2. After that, a little wooden box of dominoes and a gigantic squeeze tube of Where's Waldo? bath soap. He held the tube and read the instructions. "'Finger paint gel soap. The fun way to color yourself clean.'"

Michael cocked his head to one side, looking at Jennie with an amused, doubtful grin.

"It's red," she said in explanation to both of them. "You use it in the bathtub and you smear it all over yourself and it cleans you."

Michael raised one eyebrow, still teasing her. "You're sending this stuff to *my* house? Thanks."

"Well," she said, floundering for words. "I had bought it for mine. I thought 'why should it have to stay here?' I thought he might want to smear red around everywhere…your house, too…."

Jennie could feel the telltale signs of emotion beginning to emerge, the reddening nose, the sharpening of her voice. She had to blink rapidly, tears stung her eyes.

"Better get out of here." She kissed Cody again, this time as quickly as she could manage it, right on the end of his upturned nose. "Love you, kid."

"Love you, too, Mom. See you in two weeks."

She couldn't answer. Grief clogged her throat. She felt Michael watching her retreating figure growing smaller and smaller, the way she felt like she was growing smaller and smaller in her son's life. She wove in and out of the parked cars in the lot, looking blindly for her own. She found it at last. Only then did she hear Michael put his own car in gear and drive away.

Chapter Thirteen

Fans filled the seats around the Burn's field, settling into the ring in bright, random patterns of color. As the crowd increased, the noise and the chants rose to an echoing cacophony around them.

It was amazing that the fans had wanted to keep up with them at all, the way the team had been slumping. Five losses in a row, three of them at home, and their chances at the playoffs.

"I need a player who's willing to give me everything on the field the way you used to," Harv said. "And I don't know who that's going to be."

I do, Buddy thought, but he didn't say it. *I know exactly who.*

During the past three weeks, Buddy and Marshall Townsend had been getting together, sitting around the video room with feet propped on the coffee table, watching soccer plays. If anyone had asked him to define it, Buddy would have said they were participating in "mental exercises." But, luckily, no one had asked.

"Just don't know what's wrong with my game lately," Marshall had said, stretching lazily and crossing two arms behind his head before he settled into a new position. "I can picture you making these incredible shots. Remember that cross-field shot you made during the Galaxy game? I *dreamed* about that one."

Buddy knew how frustrating it could be when you weren't performing as well as you knew you could. Oh, did he know. But he suspected Townsend's problems stemmed from the fact that he wasn't mature enough to face the mental pressure of the game. It would come in time, though. He knew that, too.

"I picture *you* making those incredible shots. I *saw* you making them one after the other. Then I picture myself and it's just *me*."

Buddy shook his head, smiling to himself. *What a sage I am,* he thought. "Life isn't always reasonable, Marshall. So stop trying to play it out that way." How many times had Andy Kendall told him this very same thing? "You've got the right idea but you're going about it wrong."

"I am?"

"Your brain controls your body," he said simply. "If you make yourself *see* the right things, you've got it made." *If I say this to many more people,* he thought with an odd quirk of humor, *I'll end up believing it myself.*

Sports medicine, he reminded himself. This is nothing but psychological sports medicine. But Andy had used it with her kids, too.

"I learned that a while back," he said. *From someone I cared very much about.* "I think it can work for you, too." Strange that during rehabilitation after the accident, he'd forgotten so much of this.

"I'd like to try it," Marshall said. "Anything that will help me make those impossible shots."

What do I tell him now? What would Andy have told him? Buddy let his mind travel back, back before the accident, back when he had been a superstar at soccer, back when there had just been Andy.

"Come on, you!" They were skiing Breckenridge together, the snow so light and dry around his boots that it had reminded him of the flakes of dried paper he saw in all the store windows in Dallas at Christmastime. Andy'd waved at him with a wide arc of her arm. "All you do is point your skis downhill and you *go* "

"That sounds easy enough," he'd said blandly, peering down the hill. "It just doesn't *look* easy enough."

"You can do it. If it looks like you're going to run into a tree or a person, you just fall down."

"Something tells me I'm not getting the traditional ski lesson here."

"You get," she said, swinging her curly, dark ponytail at him, "exactly what you pay for."

"That's what I was afraid of." He used his poles to

push himself downhill toward her. "So I do this? Just go downhill and if I start running…into…somebody…" Here his skis passed right over hers and, as he continued on, he grabbed her tightly, hanging on to her the way a frightened child would hang on to its mother's legs. "Then I just fall…" And here she started screaming and giggling at him all at the same time, pushing him to try to get out of his grasp.

"Down…"

Kerplop. They both landed face first in the snow.

They thrashed around a bit, laughing. Andy spit snow out of her mouth. "I think I'd recommend a professional lesson," she said, deadpan. "This doesn't seem to be working."

Buddy looked at her and grinned the grin that had made him tremendously popular with female soccer fans. Her cheeks were as red as crab apples and her nose was three shades brighter. He could see two matching reflections of himself in her snow-blotched Smiths. "I think it's working just fine."

"Get off," she demanded, giggling. "Get off!"

"You aren't being very persuasive, and besides," he'd said, grinning at his own reflection in her glasses, "I don't think I can."

Their skis were so jumbled up and lying at such odd angles to each other that they would never get them untangled.

"Instructor!" she shouted from where she lay in

the snow. "Instructor! This man needs an instructor! Help! Help!"

Someone had come along soon after and had mercifully untangled them before they froze that way. After that, she had stalwartly refused to give him any more free lessons. "Enroll in a class," she told him, kissing him quickly on the lips to punctuate it. "Now. Before you kill somebody. Like me."

He had signed up immediately, and three hours later he knew how to traverse a hill and turn and draw himself to a crude, skidding stop. Rejoining Andy, Buddy persuaded her to take the lift to an intermediate hill with him. Andy had still skied circles around him. "How are you doing that?" he'd asked her.

"It's easy," she'd called back as he did his best to follow in her tracks. He was trying to decide whether it would be more fun to concentrate on his own turns or to watch the stem-christie turns she was making ahead of him.

He'd decided to match her turn for turn. He attempted to follow her but hit an icy spot, headed straight downhill and lost control. As she helped him up one more time, he realized he'd better stop concentrating on Andy's turns and start worrying about staying alive. "I tell this to the kids at Children's all the time," she'd said then. "Picture yourself doing something exactly the way you want to do it. Your brain and your body perfectly connected."

By the end of the day, he'd been able to keep up with

her. And when he got back to the Burn to start playing again, he'd found himself picturing plays, completed plays, successful goal attempts and victories.

Andy's concept was foolproof. It worked. What she had taught him meant everything to him until the accident, until he let it go.

It's funny, he thought, *that I'm sitting here beside Marshall Townsend watching tapes and trying to help him grasp the idea.* In some way, trying to get it through Marshall's head, he felt like he was teaching it to himself again.

"Marshall," he said. "I wish I could take you skiing. I think I could make you understand this if I could get you on a ski hill."

"Oh," the player said. "I ski. Had a great vacation in Vail just a couple of months ago."

"That's just it, then," Buddy said, excited now, figuring they were getting somewhere. "Control of the ball in a game of soccer is just like control of your body while you're skiing a slope. It's that brain, body, hill connection. Everything working together."

"What does a ski hill have to do with soccer?" Marshall's eyebrows narrowed. "In case you haven't noticed, our field is flat!"

"It sets the rhythm to catch, controlling the ball, trapping it and passing it. It's seeing yourself shooting past the goalie and driving in the score."

"Clear as mud, Coach!"

"Straight from research at Stanford. Your mind fires your nervous system exactly the same way as if you're actually doing it. When you picture *me* making a shot and compare that to what you think *you* can do, that screws you up, Townsend. You've got to put yourself on the line instead of working to minimize your losses."

Now, today, as Buddy stood on the edge of the playing field, his own words echoed in his mind. "Put yourself on the line instead of working to minimize your losses." But he hadn't listened to his own advice when he'd given up his career playing for the Burn. He had minimized his own losses.

No wonder Andy couldn't accept that from him. It was everything she fought against, with every child she'd ever worked with.

He pulled his cap out of his pocket and slapped it on. Marshall Townsend's opportunity could very well come on the field today. Buddy had seen the player's improvement during practice. "Harv asked me what's gotten into you," he said in the locker room as Marshall made ready for the game. "I told him that, with you, it wasn't *if* anymore. Only *when.*"

The Dallas Burn took the field at two o'clock that afternoon. As the play swung into full action, Harv and Buddy substituted players on the fly and adjusted their plans. The afternoon, as always, moved quickly. With ten minutes left to play, Spooner stole the ball from a Colorado Rapids player, quickly moving it outside, then passing right to Kirkland. Kirkland controlled the ball perfectly, moving it toward the far end of the field.

Spooner freed himself first, dancing forward with a half turn, controlled the ball and shot. Colorado's keeper deflected it with two hands high over his head. He drop-kicked it in the general direction of Marshall Townsend.

Not yet, Marshall! Buddy thought. *But almost! Almost!*

As if his friend had read his mind, Marshall dribbled the ball for five steps, looked straight toward the net and faked a shot.

Now! Buddy thought. *You've got it!*

For one moment there might as well not have been anyone or anything on the field except for Marshall, the spinning black-and-white leather ball, the Rapids' goal-keeper, the net.

"No!" Harv pounded his palm with his fist. "Not that left long shot again! *No!*"

Buddy said simply, "We've been working on this, Harv."

When Marshall took the shot, the ball shot forward half the length of the field, an inch above the ground, going at least ninety miles an hour.

The keeper dove. The ball jettisoned past him in a flash of black-and-white. It landed and lodged itself neatly in the left side of the net.

The crowd went wild.

The team went wild.

"Goal! Dallas Burn!" the announcer bellowed.

No one stopped to count how many months it had been since someone had made such an impossible shot. But Buddy knew.

"It was Townsend! Marshall Townsend!" Harv turned and gave Buddy a hard high five. "What a play! *What* a play! So help me, tonight I'm taking that boy for a New York strip dinner!"

Cody loved his new swimming class. He loved going to the big indoor pool, feeling the water all tingly and cold around him. When he was in the water, he felt almost as if he could swim. But he couldn't quite manage it, so he just pretended instead, using his hands to push and splash.

His dad had come home from the office today to bring him. There was a lady that came to his dad's house during the day to help take care of him, too. But his dad didn't spend too much time away from the house right now.

Cody liked it that Mark Kendall had introduced him to the other kids on swim team. He liked making new friends who hadn't known him before. He didn't know if his old friends at school would like him anymore since he couldn't walk around. His new friends were good because they liked him just the way he was.

In the class they took turns on a kickboard while Mark helped them splash in circles through the water. They played all sorts of water games together, diving for rings and pitching balls and closing their eyes and

looking for each other. There was a little girl named
Megan who outswam the rest of them. Somebody told
Cody that she'd won a race.

At the end of the class, his dad told him he was really
proud. He heard him say to his coach, "I believe in this
program one hundred percent. Andy's been telling us
how good it would be for Cody. But I didn't know it
would be *this* good."

"I liked it, too," Cody told his dad in the car on the way
home. "Do you think my bathing suit changes color?"

"What?"

"The pirate stuff on the seat. When it gets wet. I
think it changes color."

"I'm not sure, kiddo," his dad said, kissing him.

"Megan thinks it does. She saw a shirt that does it on
TV."

His dad smiled. "You want to go to the office with
me? This would be a good day to come, if you're not
tired. You can meet some of my patients that I always
talk about."

"Yeah, Dad! I want to—"

"Okay." His dad shifted into first gear. "We're on our
way."

When they arrived at the office, Michael introduced
Cody to Inez, the nurse, and Chris Bell, the receptionist. Cody made friends with the kids in the waiting room
and even got to sit in on one of his dad's appointments.

"This is my son, Cody," Michael said, introducing him to Bill and Marge Josephs. "I didn't think you'd mind if he sat in with us."

"Not at all," Bill bellowed in his Central Texas drawl. He said "at all" in one word. *Atall.* "You figurin' on growing up to be a doctor some day, son?"

Cody gave him a straight answer. "I don't think so. People keep asking me that question but I'm not old enough to have it all figured out yet."

"Guess what," Bill said, leaning toward him conspiratorially and pointing to the rows and rows of wrinkles around his eyes. "I'm not old enough to have it all figured out yet, either!"

"Let's get this over with, Bill," Michael said, pointing toward the examining table. "Get right on up there and let me have a look at you."

"Good luck catching him," his wife teased. "He's moving so fast these days, I have a *horrible* time catching him. I have a horrible time making him do what I want."

"Honey," Bill said. "It's all your frame of mind. When there comes the time that *I* want to do what *you* want me to do, then I'll let you catch me."

Michael shot a grin at Bill. "Been feeling good, huh?"

"The best. Like a kid. Got so much energy, I don't know what to do with it."

"Right," Marge said, winking at Cody.

"Can't decide whether to go fishing or go golfing or

go dove hunting or just hang out with the boys. And I've got these two horses named Dan and Kimbo that need riding all the time." He leaned down close to Cody. "You like to ride horses? Have your dad call me up and we'll take you out for a ride."

"Hard decisions," Marge interjected. "Too bad you don't consider fixing the doorbell as one of your heart-wrenching choices. Or how about finding the leak that's ruined all my soaps underneath the bathroom sink?"

"But, *Marge,*" he said in the exact same tone of voice Cody used when he said "But, *Mom.*" "I'm *retired.*"

"Okay. Let's check you out now," Michael said again. Bill hoisted himself up onto the table. "Good." Marge and Cody stayed silent while Michael noted Bill's blood pressure and listened to his heartbeat. "Your blood pressure's lower. Medication's working," Michael finally said. "You *are* taking them like you're supposed to? And you're following my other instructions?"

"He's doing everything you told him just like he does everything *I* tell him," Marge confirmed.

"Ma-a-arge," Bill drawled. "Don't give me away now. Yes, I'm taking those confounded pills."

"It's for your own good, you old coot," she said.

"Ma-a-arge."

Michael shook his head at both of them while Cody laughed. They put on quite a show. "Bill," he began. Then he glanced at Cody again. Cody made him see the humor here in its proper perspective. He walked over to his stubborn patient and slapped him on the back. "Bill, you're in good shape. You're eighty-four years old, you've got a heart that's getting stronger, your choles-terol level is low and it's clear that you're moving fast enough to keep Marge on her toes. I'm not going to lecture you about this, but keep the coffee down to two cups a day if you possibly can."

"I can do that, Doc," Bill said, guffawing. "I surely can."

Michael and Cody talked about Bill later on that evening on the way to Michael's first therapy session with his son. "Dad," Cody said as Michael lifted him out of the car and carried him to the gym. "That guy was funny."

"Oh, he's a character, all right."

Cody's arms clamped around the back of Michael's neck. "I liked him."

"Me, too," Michael said, glad to think of something besides the upcoming therapy. For weeks he'd wanted to be a part of this. Now that the time had come, he felt totally inept. He'd performed therapy with Cody often alone in his room. But he'd never been able to arrange his schedule so he could take part in the groups. Jennie had always done it. "A doctor's not supposed to have fa-vorites but I've got to admit Bill's one of mine. He always makes me laugh when I need it most. He's a good friend."

"His wife made me laugh, too. She ought to do like Mom. Mom always calls the plumber when we get a leak under *our* sink."

Michael's warning signals shot up. He wasn't about to let himself be drawn off in *this* direction. "Bill was very sick a while back. But he had surgery and now he's doing much better."

"Sorta like me, Dad?" Cody asked as they bobbed along.

"Yeah," Michael answered. "Sort of like you."

Andy met them in the hallway and took Cody's face in her hands. "Boy, have we missed *you* around here lately. How are things at home? How are you feeling?"

"I'm feeling real good. Dad took me to his office today and I got to meet all the patients."

Andy winked up at Michael and instantly put him at ease. "What a great way to spend your first week out of the hospital. Visiting a doctor's office."

"Oh, it was fun. I got to meet Bill Josephs and Dad checked him all over and his wife kept teasing him because he wouldn't fix things..."

Other children began gathering for the session. "Come on in, you guys," Andy called, beckoning to them. Turning back to Cody, she said, "Mark said you did *great* at swimming."

"It was fun."

Michael found a chair where he could set Cody down. For the next twenty minutes he watched while Andy showed each child how to paste funny ears and noses on pieces of paper to form faces. Next she led each of them in a rigorous clown pantomime. Michael was laughing and Cody was sweating by the time they finished.

"Now it's time for the parents to join in," Andy said, nodding at the adults. "Bring your son or daughter over here and find a comfortable place on the mats." She turned on a CD of music and instructed them. "Start with the arms. Like this."

Jennie had spent hours writing down these directions for him. He had his written instructions beside him now. But reading directions and actually performing hands-on therapy in the middle of a room full of people were two entirely different things. He grasped Cody's leg just atop the knee and began to maneuver it. He moved the leg again…again…before his son cried out. "Ouch, Dad! You're hurting me." He was shocked to see Cody biting his lip, trying to hold the tears back.

Stricken, Michael dropped Cody's leg. Around him the other parents continued to work with their children's muscles. "Cody, I'm sorry, son."

"It's okay, Dad."

A light film of sweat covered the little boy's face.

"Your mother never would have let that happen. She knows how to do this better than I do."

"Dad, don't worry. It didn't hurt that much."

"Kiddo, I'm *really* sorry."

Andy appeared at Cody's side. "Need help over here?"

"I'm hurting him," Michael said.

"Here. Let me show you." The physical therapist knelt

and took Cody's leg in two competent hands, rotating his ankle just a bit. "When you're doing a group exercise like this one, you want to work the muscle at this angle. See? Like this." The leg moved better for her, like a glider on a track, to and fro, to and fro. "Now. You try it."

"I'm afraid I'll hurt him." Oh, the great doctor who gave shots and pushed on sore muscles and gave more than his fair share of stitches! The great doctor who always said, "This won't hurt but a minute!"

"It always seems scarier than it is," Andy reassured him.

During the remainder of the session, Andy had to help him through six more exercises. That night, while Cody lay sleeping, his breath coming in light, even waves, his mouth slightly open, Michael sat staring at the wall across from him, his Bible unopened at his side. He felt ashamed of himself, that he'd fought so hard to keep Cody, that in the end it had been so easy, that he had been thinking of his own needs when Cody needed so much from him.

Father, even in following my faith, have I been relying on my own pride?

Michael knew now, more than anything, what he had to do. He waited that night until Cody's sleep became deep and heavy before he summoned the courage to telephone her. He sat in the huge chair beside the hearth and dialed the number from memory, a number that once had been his own.

It rang four times before she answered. "Hello?"

"Jennie." He hesitated. "It's me."

Total silence. Then a quick "Hello, Michael."

He didn't say anything else. He couldn't. He didn't know how to say it.

She sensed his wariness and suddenly panicked. "Michael? Is he all right? What's wrong?"

"Cody's fine, Jen. Just fine." *But no thanks to me,* he thought wryly.

She breathed a sigh of relief. "You scared me. It always scares me now when someone calls."

"I didn't mean to scare you."

His heart started pounding. Why had he done this? Why had he been so all-consumed with this crazy idea of calling her? Without confessing to her how totally inadequate he felt, he had absolutely nothing else to say. "I wish we could go back to Six Flags," he said at last.

"Me, too," she said quietly.

The silence came again. "I don't have a sense of my own competence anymore," he said. "I don't know what God is trying to show me."

"Michael." He heard it in her voice, then. She was surprised he had confessed such a thing to her.

So he opened up to her, knowing he couldn't turn back. "I got lost in the group therapy session today," he said simply. "I got into that place and I didn't know how to do anything."

Jennie set the hand towel aside, gripped the phone against her ear. "You'll do better after you practice with him." She was honestly saddened that the scheduling and the split-up of therapy had worked to Michael's disadvantage. She couldn't really picture Michael being incompetent at anything. It shocked her to hear him say he didn't know what *God* was doing. He'd always worn his newfound faith like a badge of honor. He always acted like he could do no wrong, now that he was a Christian.

He sighed, a long, lonely sound that immediately revealed to her how lost he felt.

There was no stopping it. She knew now what she would do. *He needs me,* she thought with a triumphant thrumming of her heart. *Everything else might be lost to us. But he needs me for this.*

Her question, when it came, came in a whisper as hushed as the flicker of a bird's wings. And she knew, even as she asked, that she was making herself vulnerable to him again.

"You want to go together on Friday? I could stand beside you and give you the crash Cody course."

She pictured him rocking from nervousness in his huge, comfortable recliner and now stopping, leaning forward. "What about Cody?"

"You'll have to explain to him that I'm coming to help him and not to be with you. You've got to make *sure* he understands that. Just tell him it's because you did so badly in class today and you want to do better. Tell him it's the only thing we could think of to help you."

He gave a little humph of indignation and said softly,

"I'll make sure he understands that much. We'll have a man-to-man talk."

"Be gentle with him," she said, still quietly. "That's it, then."

"Are you sure this is the best thing to do, Jennie?"

"Yes," she said, drawn by his humility, knowing full well everything she was risking. "I'm sure."

Chapter Fourteen

As Jennie stood beside the window waiting for Michael and Cody to pick her up, she felt as if she'd stepped into a bottomless chasm that might swallow her whole.

It had seemed perfect and right, though it had been difficult, when they'd spent time together at the hospital and made decisions for Cody when he was ill. Today, however, signaled a new phase in their relationship with each other, and with their son. Today each of them would stand in the other's territory, side by side, and Cody would see them doing it.

She started when she saw the BMW round the corner. She grabbed her purse, trying to quiet the loud thudding of her heart.

"Hey, Mom!" Cody called as she climbed in behind him.

"How are ya, kid?" she asked, kissing him. "You

look bigger than you looked the other day." She glanced at Michael's reflection in the rearview mirror. She saw the gratefulness in his eyes and didn't know how to respond. "Are you two ready for this?"

"Yep!" Cody said happily.

"As ready as I'll ever be," Michael agreed. And Jennie decided that Michael sounded happy, too.

"Good."

Cody jabbered all the way to the hospital. He talked about swimming and spending the night with Taylor and his new friends at the pool. He talked about the golden Labrador puppy, Jehosophat, who had moved in next door.

Jennie started worrying. Cody seemed far too animated. Was he again hoping that she and Michael would reconcile?

The drive to the hospital seemed an eternity. When they finally arrived at the gym, and had set Cody down to visit with his friends before class, she cornered Michael. "Did you talk to him?"

"I did."

"What did you say?"

"You want to know how our talk went? I told him as best I could that we had an old, deep connection between us, because we had *him* together, a child we both loved.

"I told him that it was right, sensible, that we would be together to support him. I told *him* it was good for us to treat each other as old friends. That it should make him feel safe." *And that's what they were doing, weren't they?*

"Good," she said. "I didn't know exactly how you were going to put it."

They started back toward the group of children and parents. "I wanted to make sure he understood," Michael said, searching her face for any reaction.

Yes, yes, her face seemed to tell him. *You said all the right things.*

For Jennie, it was a welcome reprieve to begin working with Cody again. When it came time for the parents to participate, Michael carried Cody over to the mats. Then he stepped back so Jennie could work with him. She motioned to Michael to squeeze in next to her.

"I'll show you how," she whispered as he felt a rush of gratitude for her. "It's a snap. You'll get the hang of it and you'll be the best one here."

"There isn't much chance of that."

"Oh, yes there is."

The first few exercises went well. Michael learned the correct angle and placement of Cody's feet, hips and knees. But as Jennie began to work with Cody's arms, she could feel him tightening up against her. "Hey," she said to Cody as Michael looked on. "What are you doing? Your muscles are getting tight, little one."

"It hurts, Mom."

"You've got to push ahead through this part."

She felt Michael's reassuring hand on her back. She

closed her eyes and sat back on her heels, easing into his touch, forgetting for a moment where she was, who she was, who *he* was.

Oh. And suddenly, as she thought it, she realized it felt almost like a prayer. *What would it feel like to always have something like this in my life? Something to support me?*

For the rest of the session, the three of them laughed and told jokes. And, as they drove home together, Cody fell fast asleep in the back seat of the car.

They drove on in silence, but this time the silence felt comfortable between them. Michael pulled the car up in front of her house. Before Jennie had time to reach for the handle, he'd parked the car and jumped out.

"It's not dark. And this isn't a date. You don't have to walk me to the door."

"I want to."

She climbed out. He strolled with her up the walk and waited while she dug her keys out of her bag. When she turned to thank him, he grasped her forearms with gentle, certain hands. "Jennie. Please—"

"Michael—" She glanced back at the car and saw Cody sleeping there, his lashes resting against his cheeks as lightly as gauze. "I don't think—"

He held up a hand, stopping her words. "You have to know this," he said, persisting. "You have to know how much I needed you today. You have to know how much it meant that you came."

"I think I know." Their eyes met in the growing darkness.

He gave her a half smile, a bittersweet smile made more melancholy because he tilted his head at her like their little boy. Then, without another word he drew her close, his arms tightening warm and strong around her.

"I just wanted to do this again," he whispered. He held her as he had never held her before, like a drowning man seizing a life raft. "Oh, Jen, I've missed you."

"Me, too."

Their eyes met again and held in the dimness of the porch light. As though it were the most natural thing in the world, as though it weren't the very thing they'd been fighting so fiercely, he took her into his arms and kissed her for a long, long time. When he stopped, they were both breathless.

"Should I tell you I'm sorry?" He searched her face.

"What is this?" she asked him. "What is this?" She stopped. "It isn't what you told Cody. It isn't just *old friends*."

For minutes after that, they stood fiercely entwined, not moving, Jennie burying her face against Michael's chest, where she could hear his breath. And even after he drove away and she stood there alone, she could still feel the strong, steady beating of his heart.

Jennie cleaned all day when it came time for Cody to move back in with her. She nervously dawdled around the house, straightening things she'd already straightened twice, rearranging pillows on the sofa, pausing in the doorway to Cody's room and just looking at it.

Michael arrived at five-thirty. "Hi, you two!" She held the door open for them. "I thought you'd never get here." She ruffled Cody's hair. "It's about time you started hanging around this place again."

"I'll be glad to be hanging around this place, too."

She looked up and past her son's head. "Hello, Michael."

"Hello, Jennie."

"Can I see my room?" Cody asked.

"Sure," Jennie told him.

"Here," Michael said, bending to lift him.

Jennie touched Michael's elbow. "No. Let me try."

"You sure you want to?"

She nodded. She'd have to carry him around plenty soon enough. She might as well start while Michael could help her.

He stood behind her while she gave Cody a tight, giant hug and lifted him. "Agh," she groaned, teasing him. "You've been growing again!"

"I'm trying to grow!"

They made it up the hallway without knocking the walls down. They only ran into two things, a watercolor painting of bluebonnets that swung crazily on the wall when they bumped it, and Lester the cat, who squalled as if he'd been mortally wounded when Jennie stepped on his tail.

"Oh, Lester," she sighed. "I didn't even know you were down there."

She plunked Cody down on his bed and propped pillows all around him.

She stood back, giving him some room. "You want us to stay with you?"

"Naw. I just wanted to come in here and remember everything."

"Okay." She wasn't certain she and Michael should go. "You'll call me if you need me?"

"I'll call you."

"He'll be okay," Michael reassured her. Then he turned to his son. "I guess I'll go, Cody."

"Okay, Dad. Thanks."

He bent down on his knees. "You be good for Mom, you hear?"

"I will."

"You'll remember everything we talked about?"

Cody nodded.

"Okay. Love you, son."

"Love you, too, Dad."

This was the hardest part for both of them, telling him goodbye.

Jennie followed Michael along the hallway. "You're going to miss him, aren't you?"

"Terribly."

He turned to face her. He had nothing else to say but he couldn't quite bring himself to leave.

"Can I come pick him up and continue to take him to Andy's sessions?" he asked.

"You want to?" she said, surprised. She'd figured that, with Cody gone, he'd go back to spending long hours with his patients and at the hospital.

"I *do* want to," he said. "We've been doing fine in there—" he shot her a sheepish grin "—now that I know what I'm doing. Thanks for coming with us."

She turned and looked out the window at nothing. "You're welcome."

He watched her for a moment. Then he stepped up behind her. "Jennie? What is it? What's the matter?"

"Nothing."

"It isn't nothing. I can tell."

"Why do you try to read my mind?" she asked. "Why do you think you know me so well?"

"Because I do," he told her. "We were married once. I can't help it." Then he asked her very quietly, "Are you afraid to have Cody here?"

She turned slowly to face him. "I am." Then she took a deep breath and said in a rush, "I fought so hard for this."

He touched her on the chin. "You'll do fine."

As she watched the man who had been such an integral part of her life for so long, she realized she wasn't being completely honest. "There's more to it than that, Michael. It's more than Cody. It's you. I'm realizing that, when I'm afraid, I'm depending on you. I've started *needing* you again."

"No," Michael said quietly. "No. You mustn't think it. It isn't me you need." She looked a question at him. "You're Cody's mother. And, beneath it all—" here he paused and seemed to struggle with himself "—beneath it all, I don't think God could have picked anybody better for the job."

For no reason at all, at Michael's words, Jennie remembered one fall when they'd gone to East Texas to cut firewood and they'd tumbled around on the ground in the acorns. She remembered their first little apartment in Dallas. She remembered watching him sleep one of the last nights they'd been together, his back an insurmountable mountain that marked his edge of the bed, when she had thought, "I don't know him anymore. And he doesn't know me."

I don't think God could have picked anyone better than you for the job.

It isn't me you need.

If it wasn't Michael, what had brought her to this point of aching, to this feeling that something had to be lacking.

I KNOW THE PLANS I HAVE FOR YOU.

After all that had gone before between her and Michael, how could she have felt so free to tell him what she needed?

PLANS TO PROSPER YOU AND NOT TO HARM YOU. PLANS TO GIVE YOU HOPE AND A FUTURE.

Jennie didn't know where the sudden sense of desperation came from as the Bible verse came to mind. This sudden sense of something tugging at her heart. She'd gotten Cody here; she'd gotten what she needed.

It isn't me you need, Michael had said.

What was it then?

The way I feel, God never would have picked me for this. God never would have picked me for any job.

She couldn't help wondering now, though, after Michael's words. Something inside her yearned to ask, *What if he's right? What if there's more?*

Chapter Fifteen

When Jennie started drawing again, she made funny sketches for Cody and jotted down stories. Tonight she started drawing caricatures of Cody's new friends on the swim team. Cody watched, entranced, while she shaded them in.

"The swimming has really helped you, Bear." She scrubbed the paper with a dull pencil. "Look. Here's you. Here's your fabulous new bathing suit with pirate flags."

"That's great, Mom!"

"Sometimes I wish I could do something more to help. All these other people are helping *you...*"

"I bet you could help. I bet you could help Mark get more kickboards so we could invite more kids."

"You don't have enough kickboards?"

"No. We have to wait *forever* to get a turn on them."

"If Mark had more children, could he purchase more supplies?"

"Nope," Cody said. "We always gripe about taking turns. Mark says he doesn't have money for everything he needs."

Jennie had heard about the tax cuts and the programs that had been affected; it hadn't seemed like anything more than a news story to her when she had worked at the paper. And suddenly, as she sat sketching, what had once seemed like an impersonal news item now hit in the vicinity of her heart.

I could make a difference. I know I could.

After Cody went to bed, she telephoned Andy, her heart thumping with excitement. "Would Mark let me organize some sort of fund-raiser? The *Times-Sentinel* is always looking for public service projects to be involved in."

Andy's voice brightened. "Oh, Jennie. If he had the resources, there are so many more things he could do. He could reach more kids. He could buy more equipment. Would you really do something like that?"

"I'll phone Art first thing Monday morning and then I'll talk to Mark when I take Cody to swimming," Jennie told her. "Consider it done."

Harv Siskell retired from the Dallas Burn in the middle of the season with a huge party and a five-tiered cake. Buddy Draper, this came as no surprise to anyone, was named his replacement. Buddy's career as head coach of the Burn had begun.

On the morning he was scheduled to coach his first game by himself, Buddy stood on the field midway between the two goals, having pulled his zippered satin jacket more snugly around him, his hands jammed into the pockets. The sun was just riding up over the Dallas skyline and, outside, the day was frigid, one of those wet winter days in Dallas that makes you feel the cold deep down to your bones.

Buddy crossed the huge field alone, the soles of his shoes whispering against the grass as he made his way to the half line. In seven hours, the stands would be full again and he'd embark on yet another new phase in his life. He had already come so far now, he could scarcely remember what it felt like to be a star player.

He looked to the left and the right, running the game plan through his mind, hoping he had considered everything, and that he could make Harv proud.

Buddy loved game days more than anything. Each game day was like taking a big test—one you passed every time you won.

He went into his office and tried to convince himself that this was just another game, that no one would remember it, that it didn't matter that this was his first outing as a professional head coach. But, try as he might, he couldn't manage to relax.

By the time the fans began to arrive and find their

seats, a little bit after noon, Buddy felt like a fish out of water, gasping for breath.

Today they were scheduled to play the San Jose Earthquakes. The Earthquakes were already in their locker room, laughing with camaraderie, when Buddy headed down the hallway to find his team. When he walked in, they were all waiting for him.

"Here's Coach!" someone hollered.

"We've got to make this happen for Draper!" someone else shouted.

Marshall Townsend pitched him one of the practice balls. "So do you want the game ball today, Coach?" he asked with a wide grin on his face.

"Only if we win."

He gathered them into a group and outlined his game plan for the day. He talked about effort, passing, control. It was everything Harv Siskell had always talked to him about, everything that had once made a difference in his life. That and the positive thoughts Andy had shared with him.

Andy. How many times had he thought of her lately? How many times he had wondered if she'd come to watch him again at one of the games. Every week, thousands of people cheered for him and his team. Every week he pretended to himself that one of the fans might be her, that she might be ready to forgive him, that she might be willing to accept the decisions he'd made.

Just before game time, he and the Burn gathered in

a big circle, put their right hands together and bellowed, "Go, Burn!" as they lifted fists to the sky. The crowd roared as they raced out onto the field. And, after a few minutes of raucous warm-ups, the clock just below the huge MSL banner read 2:00 p.m.

The Earthquakes took possession of the ball for the kick-off at center line. For the next forty-five minutes, the players crisscrossed the field in wild patterns, the striker made two shots, the keepers switched places and the press drove Buddy nuts. He felt as if they never took the cameras off him during the first half. He needed to concentrate on the game and on what to tell his players. Then Marshall Townsend passed the ball with a one-touch shot when he should have controlled it.

"Get over here," Buddy said to his player after authorizing a substitution. "It looks like school-yard soccer out there."

"Sure, Coach." Marshall shot him a grin. "You sound like Harv."

"I'm *supposed* to sound like Harv."

Marshall reentered the game three minutes later. As the last period began, the scoreboard read San Jose 4, Dallas 3.

An Earthquakes player belted the ball toward the Burn's goal, but once again the keeper blocked it. He punted it to the right side of the field, where the San Jose forward trapped it. Two steps forward, and he crossed it to a player on the left side.

When Marshall got the ball he, too, trapped it, jealously controlling it himself for several steps before he passed it backward to the defender. The defender in turn passed the ball back to the right forward. And Dallas's right forward, Eric Spooner, took the shot.

San Jose's keeper blocked the ball with his fist. The ball barely missed the outside post and rebounded. Chuck Kirkland was right beneath it, already anticipating its return pattern. The ball shot through the air several feet above the ground. As Buddy watched with clenched fists, he knew the only thing Kirkland could do was volley it.

The left forward sprang from the ground like a giant cat, whipping his foot out in a fierce kick that sent the high ball straight back into the goal like a guided missile.

Score. Dallas.

Fans jumped up and down in the stands, hugging each other and cheering. The television cameras from WFAA and KTVT moved in ever closer. But with three minutes left in the game, while one of the Burn's best defenders sat waiting in the penalty box, San Jose turned the tide by scoring again.

The Burn and Buddy couldn't recover from that. When the last whistle blew at 4:25 that Saturday afternoon, the score stood San Jose 5, Dallas 4.

"Buddy Draper?" The sports reporter from Channel 11 called to him as he started toward the locker room. "You got time for a short interview?"

"Certainly," he agreed. He spent five minutes with the reporter, telling the people watching he thought his team had expended too much energy early, and that perhaps the players had placed too much weight on the game because it was his first. He was pleased with his players' performances and told everyone so. And, just as the cameraman changed to a different angle and the reporter asked one last question, Marshall Townsend loped up beside him. "Guess you don't want the game ball since we lost, huh?"

Buddy wasn't sure how to answer that. The cameras glinted at him. He turned away to collect his thoughts. And that's when he saw her. Andy stood ten rows above him wearing a red dress that looked vaguely familiar, her dark hair lying in soft curls around her shoulders, her eyes meeting his just as he'd always imagined they would after he'd caught that one glimpse of her so long ago, every game, from any place in the stands.

He forgot Marshall's question. He forgot the sports reporter from KTVT. He even forgot the cameras and the mike shoved practically against his chin. "Andy?" he called out. *"Andy?"*

She pattered down the steps toward him, looking mildly surprised and even a little unnerved by his reaction.

The camera cut away. "Hey, stranger," she said, grinning, as she leaned over the railing and took his hand. "It's nice to see you."

"You, too."

"You still give interviews, I see," she said quietly.

"Don't know about that." He smiled. "What are you doing here?"

She shrugged. "I just—needed to know how you were doing."

"I'm doing fine."

"I know that. I—mean—I would have known that from all the stories I've read. Marshall Townsend is doing a good job taking your place. He's one of the best strikers I've seen."

"He's gotten better." *Thanks to you,* Buddy thought. But he didn't dare say it. He asked what he thought was a safer question. "This your first game this season?"

She shook her head. "No. I've come to several."

Chuck Kirkland came out to find him. "Coach. We're waiting in the locker room."

He searched Andy's eyes wordlessly.

"Go ahead," she said, taking one step back. "I shouldn't keep you."

"Thanks for coming," he said. "It means a lot."

"Buddy." She said it so softly he almost couldn't hear her. "It's good to see you."

The players surrounded him, moving him toward the lockers. He couldn't say any more to her. But just as he entered the locker room, he caught one last glance of her as she stood high in the stands, gathering her jacket, watching him.

"So? What did you think?" Marshall asked, teasing

him the moment he arrived back with the team. "Are we gonna have to throw this game ball into the trash? Or are you gonna take it home?"

Andy didn't think I trusted myself enough. But I've trusted God to show me a new path.

He held out his hand for the game ball.

"Good effort, guys," he told them all. "It's an afternoon I'll remember my whole life. Thanks."

He spun the ball high into the air, and caught it.

Jennie called Art Sanderson first thing Monday morning. It didn't take her long to convince him that the *Times-Sentinel* should be a corporate sponsor for the swim team fund-raiser. Art discussed it with the marketing staff and called her back almost immediately.

"We like it," he said. "How much will you be willing to do for this? Are you going to organize it? What do you have in mind?"

"I'm thinking of doing a variety show that spotlights the kids on the team," Jennie explained. "We'll have musical numbers and skits interspersed with appearances by several Dallas celebrities."

"What celebrities are you thinking of?"

Jennie thought about it. "I'll have to talk to several and see who's willing. I was thinking Tony Romo from the Cowboys. Some local DJs. Maybe a few Ranger players and someone from the Burn and the weatherman from Channel 8."

"Let us know what you come up with. When it comes time for publicity, the *Times-Sentinel* will handle it."

"I'd like to do some drawings for the ads," Jennie said. "We can print up posters, too. I'll donate any artwork you need. I've got some great drawings of the swim team."

"What about music?" Art asked her. "I assume we'll need that, too."

"Let me talk to somebody at the symphony," Jennie suggested. "I'll bet we can get some of the instrumentalists to donate their time."

"When you're finished with this major project," Art said conspiratorially. "Maybe you'll consider coming back to work."

"Ha." She gave a little laugh. She'd been wondering when he was going to bring that up again. "I don't know, Art. Don't count on it. I've got accustomed to staying around the house with this little boy."

Art shook his head in frustration. "You know I had to try."

Michael sat at the huge table in Marge Josephs's kitchen. "What a great breakfast, Marge," he said, leaning back and patting his belly. "It's been a long time since I've eaten like that." Everything had been delicious. Fresh grapefruit from the Texas Rio Grande Valley. Venison sausage from the deer Bill had brought in last fall. An omelet filled with tomatoes and green peppers and onions from the Josephses' garden out back.

"Well, Doc," Bill said. "We wanted to do something nice for you. You've done so much for us. And breakfast is our best meal of the day."

"I believe that," Michael said.

"Come on out back," Bill said, scooting his chair from the table. "Come see my horses."

Michael followed Bill out through the screened-in porch and past about a hundred old fishing rods. They walked out through a rickety grape arbor to the corral. When Bill whistled, the horses whinnied and came running. "This here's Dan. And this mare is Kimbo. Anytime you want to use these horses and go riding, Doc, let me know. That boy of yours looks like he'd make a fine rider. They need somebody to exercise 'em."

"Cody's ridden some. His mother loves horses."

"His mother can ride, too. Kimbo's a fine horse for a woman." Bill stopped and cocked his head at Michael. "You divorced from that boy's mother? I heard somebody talking about that."

Michael nodded. "It's been four years now."

"Too bad," Bill said. "Too bad. Ain't nothin' better than living with a good woman, Michael. Makes you live a *long time* having somebody like Marge taking care of you. I recommend it highly."

"Yeah." Michael slapped him on the back. "But you said somebody like *Marge.*"

They went up to the barn, where Bill showed Michael his chickens and his rabbits. "I keep the rabbits around here for the grandkids," he said. "They're more fun than the cats. The cats out here go wild. The kids can't get their hands on them."

After a final tour of the house that included a long description with photos of the Josephses' grandchildren, Michael was ready to leave. He hugged Marge goodbye. "You're the best," he told her. "I don't know of any other doctor who's as lucky as I am."

"Morning, Bear." Jennie hugged Cody in his bed. "How'd you sleep?"

He said. "I dreamed you and Dad took me to the fair."

"We did that once. When you were a little boy. We took you to the Texas State Fair. You ate a corn dog and threw up."

"I'm sure glad I didn't dream that part," he said, laughing.

"It was a bad dream," she teased him. "Believe me."

For breakfast, she settled him in his chair, gave him a steaming mug of cocoa and a bowl of oatmeal. Then she perched across the breakfast bar from him. "I talked to Art Sanderson this morning, my editor from the newspaper, and we're going to do a big show to help your swim team."

"Are you serious? That will be *great!* Can I be in the show?"

"You sure can."

"You think Dad will come and see it?"

"I know he will. He'll be so proud of you, he won't be able to keep away."

Jennie brought up the next subject with great care; she didn't know how Cody would feel about it.

"We've got to go to the hospital today. Andy wants you to come to a special class."

"What kind of class?" Cody whined. "I'm so sick of the hospital."

Jennie took both of his hands in hers. "It's a class so you can learn to use a wheelchair."

"I don't need that. I don't need a wheelchair."

"I think you do, darling. Just for a little while."

"No."

She couldn't believe her ears. "Cody—"

"I don't want to go."

As she dressed him that morning, she knew he was still angry with her. But she had no choice. He was getting heavier for her to carry every day.

"My legs are working *fine*," he said to her as she adjusted him in the car. "I've worked so hard. What do they think? That I'm really never going to walk again?"

"That isn't it at all," Jennie said, fighting back panic.

"You're getting one of those chairs because you've given up on me."

Andy did her best to reason with him when they arrived. "You'll be able to get around the house better. You won't have to depend on your mom and dad for so many things. You can even go back to school."

A nurse pushed the chair in to them. It was entirely different from what Jennie had expected. It folded out, was lightweight, had red metal arms and a bright striped canvas seat. "Cody," Jennie said. "It's great! Look at it. Everybody at school will want you to give them rides on this thing."

"No." Cody was gritting his teeth, his face beet red. "Get Dad. Mom, get Dad. *He* won't make me do this."

Jennie wanted to shriek at him. *This isn't fair! Your dad is the one who thinks you ought to have surgery! Surgery that could make you worse off than you are! Dad's at his office.*

"Dad will not make me sit in that thing like I'm a sick person."

"You aren't a sick person." *Oh, Cody,* she thought. "You're a healthy little boy who's getting closer and closer to walking every day."

"Dad!" he kept hollering. "Get my Dad!"

Chapter Sixteen

No amount of maneuvering or cajoling on Jennie's part was going to get Cody into that chair. Andy tried, too, and so did one of the interns. But Cody sat there, crying, stubborn as a mule, and refused to unbend his legs. He would have fallen to the floor if he had to so he could prove his point. Thirty minutes later, exhausted and defeated, Jennie finally telephoned Michael.

"I'm sorry," the receptionist told her. "He's with a patient right now. Can I have him call you back?"

"No." Jennie was past the point of exhaustion and disappointment, and was almost ready to break. *Isn't it funny?* she thought. *I've handled so many big things with Cody. And it's this little thing—this one day—this chair—that's going to break me.*

"This is Jennie Stratton. You have to interrupt him." She didn't identify herself further. She didn't want to say "his ex-wife." But she couldn't say "his wife." "Can you get him on the phone now, please?"

The receptionist sounded dubious. "You may have to wait a while."

"I'll wait as long as I need to," she said.

She waited in Andy's office for fifteen minutes. She could still hear Cody crying in the next room. Every three minutes or so, the receptionist came back on the line and asked her, "Do you want to *continue* holding?" and she'd say yes.

Then finally, finally, she heard his voice on the other end of the line. "Jen? Is it you? What's wrong?"

"It's me."

The sound of his voice almost made her crumple with relief.

"What is it?"

"I need you. I don't know what to do." She told him about the chair. "I don't know whether Cody's scared he can't do it right or whether he thinks we don't believe in him anymore. Or maybe he thinks we're pushing him back into things too fast."

"Why don't you ask him?"

"I'm not sure he could answer even if I asked the right questions." She could still hear Cody crying through the closed door. "He keeps asking for you and saying *you* wouldn't make him do this."

"I *would*."

"What if I bring him to the phone? I could try to calm him down enough so he could listen to you."

"No," Michael said. "I'm coming down there. I'll cancel everything for the afternoon. You stick with him and tell him I'm on my way."

True to his word, Michael arrived within the half hour, still dressed in his doctor's coat and the little plastic badge that said Michael Stratton, M.D. He walked immediately toward Cody, stopping only long enough to squeeze Jennie's arm in a gesture of support.

"What's the problem, son?" He stooped down beside Cody.

"I—don't—want—one—of—those—chairs—I—want—to—wa-a-a-lk—" Cody wailed.

"You think if we get you in a chair that we'll stop helping you learn to walk again?" Michael asked.

"Yes. That's what I think."

"That isn't what we'll do at all."

"I—don't—want—one—of—those—chairs—" Cody said through clenched teeth.

"Your mom and I have gotten you this far. You've got to trust us a bit, okay?"

"I—knew—you—wouldn't—make—me—do—this."

Little rivulets of tears ran down Cody's cheeks and Michael handed him a tissue. "Tell me, Cody, when is the last time you wanted to take the easy way out of something? That isn't what you need right now. You've got to try a few new things." Cody blew his nose.

Michael turned to Andy. "Can you have someone bring in a chair that's big enough for me?"

"That I can do, Dr. Stratton."

Michael eased himself into the chair as soon as the hospital aide brought it, strapped himself in with the seat belt, and began to manipulate the big, shiny wheels. He went the wrong way at first and winked at Jennie. "I've never actually *done* this before."

"I didn't figure you had," Jennie said.

"Dad," Cody said, smiling in spite of himself. "You're being goofy."

Michael kept spinning. "This is fun." He made himself woozy.

Jennie was getting dizzy just watching him.

"Actually," Cody commented, still dubious, "that looks like it *could* be fun."

"It is," Michael said, grinning. "But, better than that, look how fast I can go." He shot across the room as fast as he could until he came nose-to-nose with the little boy. "And I can stop on a dime."

Jennie treasured what Michael was doing for their son. Her emotion was so reassuring, so *certain*, that she didn't even try to chase it away.

It would be so easy, she thought, *to fall in love with this man again.*

"Come here," Michael said, holding his arms out to Cody. "Let's try this together. I'll let you work the wheels, okay?" He unfastened his own seat belt and lifted Cody with ease. "There you go."

They sat in the chair together with Cody at the controls, turning the wheels carefully so the shiny spokes moved opposite each other just the way Michael had showed him. Michael whispered something in his ear and, all of a sudden, Cody made the chair shoot forward. Together they banged into the wall.

"No!" Michael said, laughing, as they backed away from the wall and gave it another shot. "No reckless driving or I want off of this thing!"

"Oh, Dad." In a new singsong voice. "Chicken!"

"I'm not a chicken. I'm just smart. If you're going to drive like that, you get your own chair." He motioned toward the bright little chair that stood ready, waiting for Cody.

Jennie thought her heart would burst as she stooped down toward Michael to unfasten her son from the big chair. As she hugged Cody to her, she felt so close to his father that she said impulsively, "With you teaching him to drive, we'd better take out extra insurance."

He looked her straight in the eye, deathly serious. "I don't know of any company around that would consider us a good risk."

No. A bad risk at driving. A bad risk at marriage. She looked straight back at him. "I'm sure you're right." *We aren't a good risk. We never were. But I think we're changing.*

When Michael turned back to Cody, he said, "Just because of this chair, you mustn't think either your mother or I have given up on you. We're together on doing what's best for you, do you understand that?"

It occurred to Jennie that if God was in the business of answering prayers, that He had just answered one.

And with her ex-husband's words of support, Jennie's questions about God, her feelings about Michael, didn't seem so staggering anymore.

She lifted Cody, and Andy held the chair steady while she lowered him into it. As soon as they had him buckled in, Cody and his father shot out the door like streaks, shouting about racing each other up the hallway.

It wasn't about choosing sides anymore, Michael kept thinking as he hurried through his daily routine, treating patients, checking e-mail, having his nurse follow up with his clients after they went home, doing his on-call at the hospital. It was about Jennie and him keeping a firm foundation of love beneath Cody. Because of everything that had happened in the past months, that seemed to be getting easier and easier.

Is she beginning to see You, Father?

Michael didn't know what had happened to change Jennie's heart, and she seemed different to him, more confident, more joyous. But one evening when he stopped by to check on Cody, he saw that she had an invitation to a Bible study on the kitchen counter.

"What's this?" he asked, picking it up tentatively.

"Oh, that." She shrugged as if it meant nothing. "It's something Andy goes to. She thought I might like it."

"Are you going to go?" He searched her face dubiously.

"I went." She turned to him, smiling. "It was yesterday."

Michael didn't dare ask more questions. He didn't want her to think he was hounding her or trying to make her tell him her thoughts. He laid the invitation down and turned to go in search of Cody.

But Jennie said, "The last time I was in a church was the day we got married, did you know that? Do you remember how pretty that little place was? With all those candles and the flowers and the light streaming in all those colored windows?"

Michael *did* remember. He remembered the huge bell hanging in the front steeple. He remembered the redbud trees practically groaning with pink blossoms lining the walk. He remembered the wedding vows he had recited to her.

How long ago all of that had been.

"I remember."

"Remember your cousin—what was his name—threw the ring pillow at you like it was a football?"

Michael couldn't help laughing. "I don't remember that part. I just remember my brother cracking up because the flower girl picked her nose when she walked up the aisle."

She gave him a little slap. "Men and their humor. That part I *had* forgotten."

"That's the real-life stuff," he told her. "That's the stuff that makes everything good."

The next Tuesday, while Michael served his on-call at the hospital, he made a detour to the cafeteria. As he slid his tray along the chrome rail and reached for an orange, he glanced across the room and saw Andy buying a copy of the *Morning News*. She didn't take a seat; she shook open one of the sections and scanned the pages as if in search for one article.

When he came up behind her, he saw her reading the sports section.

"Looking for soccer stories?" he teased her.

Andy clutched the paper shut. He saw her blushing.

"The Burn did well last night. They beat the Metrostars."

"So I was reading." And then she laughed.

"Andy." And suddenly Michael didn't know how to say it, so great was the emotion that settled on his heart. How had so much time gone by, and he had not thought to say this to her? "Andy, I don't even know where to start."

Her brows narrowed. Her smile widened a touch. He could tell she couldn't guess what he wanted to say.

"What is it, Dr. Stratton?"

"I'm just so…grateful." His throat constricted. He almost couldn't get the last word out. "For the work you've done with my son. For the friend you're being to my ex-wife."

She laid the newspaper aside and, by the smile she shot him, he knew he'd surprised her.

"Thank you," he said. "For everything."

He could see her looking to wave it off, trying to find a way to say, *but it's my job. It doesn't matter.*

He said, "No. You have to accept this, my *gratitude.* It's important for both of us."

So she did. "You're welcome. People don't often say 'thank you' here," she said. "They're so stressed." She laughed again. "But then, I don't need to tell you that."

Michael picked up the orange and began to peel it, as if he was unwrapping a gift. "Gratitude is a powerful, healing emotion. I'm learning that." He offered Andy a half, she took a segment of it, before he popped the rest of it in sections in his mouth and made his way back to the E.R.

Michael's on-call night was typically eventful. The nurses running triage. The waiting room busting at the seams.

A man came in for stitches because someone had broken a glass on his face in a nightclub. A man who told his daughter he'd hit himself with a hammer actually had a needle broken off and buried in his arm. A woman had started premature labor and he admitted her to a room right away.

Then came the teenager who needed wrist surgery because he'd fallen off a skateboard going way too fast and had shattered his growth plate.

When Michael called the orthopedic surgeon to come in, he got Dr. Phillips. As the surgical tech brought in the sterile instruments Dr. Phillips requested and the two of them washed up at the sink, the woman surgeon asked through her mask, "How's that boy of yours doing?"

Michael's hands paused beneath the stream of water. He didn't know why, but he felt uneasy. He wanted to focus on the teen with the green hair who was, at this very moment, going under anesthesia.

He snapped his gloves on and held his hands high and cupped, ready for this next task. "Cody's making slow progress," he answered at last. "We're proud of him. He's working hard."

The patient's vital signs had steadied to a deep, rhythmic pattern on the electronic monitor. Somewhere in the background, Michael heard the sound of the automated blood-pressure cuff sighing out its air.

"You know, he got that reprieve from the muscle surgery," Dr. Phillips said as she examined this other boy under the bright light. "I had the chance to see your son's chart the other day."

Michael couldn't keep the surprise from his voice. "You did?"

"Yes. I've been keeping an eye on him." Dr. Phillips held out her hand; the surgical tech placed a knife there.

"If you can convince your ex-wife, I'd like to go ahead and loosen that muscle."

With that they went into the surgery. Michael assisted Dr. Phillips with a sudden, unexpected anger rising in his veins.

Michael had never told anyone, but he prayed for his patients as he worked on them. Tonight, while Dr. Phillips opened the boy's arm and rearranged pieces of ligament and fragmented bone, Michael found himself too out-of-temper to do that. He watched while Adele Phillips's adept hands positioned a metal plate between two delicate bones.

When she stepped back to survey her work, she told him offhandedly, "You'll be looking at some real hip problems for your son later if you don't take my advice."

"If you think we still ought to go ahead with the surgery," Michael prompted her. "That means...?"

"I think he's made all the progress he's going to make."

How could she say that? She hadn't seen Andy and Jennie taking him through his paces. She hadn't seen Cody eyeing his wheelchair with fear, Cody asking, Does this mean you're giving up on me?

They worked side by side for another hour. When Dr. Phillips stepped back and indicated she wanted Michael to complete the stitches, Michael did so with sharp, terse movements. He felt angrier with himself than he did with Adele Phillips, and he didn't understand why. When they met again over the sink after the patient had been taken to recovery, Michael said, "We doctors think we have all the answers, don't we?"

Dr. Phillips said, "At some point, Dr. Stratton, you're going to have to accept the fact that your son isn't going to walk again."

Michael halted.

"Your ex-wife doesn't know what she's talking about when she fights against it," Dr. Phillips continued. "You know, we're guided by science. She's letting her emotions guide her instead."

Suddenly Michael realized what he had been wrong about, wallowing every day as he had been in his own indecision and his hurt. He had been living in his own power, in his hopes for himself and Jennie, in his own need to stay in control.

Help me, Father. Show me the next step.

He turned to his colleague and, when he spoke, his words came in an angry growl. "I know the power of words, Doctor," he told her. "Believe me, I've spoken them over plenty of folks, too.

"Believe me, I know the power of spoken destiny. Tell me it's going to be a battle with Cody—I already know that. But don't tell me the end result because that's up to God."

Oh, Father. I wanted You to work in Jennie's heart. When all the time, You wanted to work in mine.

Michael yanked off his protective cap and took off his protective booties.

The next steps—the words came into his heart, seemingly put there the way someone places a clock on a shelf—*are Cody's steps.*

Michael straightened, gripped on to those words with joy. "I stand behind Jennie's decision," he told Dr. Phillips. "We have heard your opinion and we respect it. The next thing we're going to do is pray."

Bill Josephs sat on the examining table and bit his lip while Michael listened to his chest. "There's not anything wrong with me, Doc," Bill said finally. "I know those pains came from something I ate for dinner last night."

"You can't be too careful," Michael told him as he moved around to his back and listened to a different area.

"Marge keeps sending me over here. I hiccup and she tells me I need to see you. Frankly, I think she has a crush on you. That's why she always insists I come to this place."

Michael stood up and let his stethoscope drop to his chest. He couldn't hear Bill's heart anymore anyway; he couldn't listen to the thumping of a patient's heart and the patient's opinion about things all at the same time. And Bill Josephs had plenty of opinions about everything. Instead, Michael smoothed his hair back exaggeratedly. He knew exactly how to get his old friend's goat.

"You think Marge really likes me, Bill? Is that why she had me out for breakfast? You know, if it wasn't for her bringing you in all the time, I wouldn't have a practice at all. You and Marge are the only reason I can pay all my bills."

"I'm that way to everybody," the old guy said, winking. "That's why my momma named me *Bill*. You should *see* all my bills. During my lifetime, I've kept half of this country in business. I've got this nightmare I get to heaven and an angel hands me a list of all my charges. Please pay in advance."

Michael chuckled. "It could happen." He flipped Bill's chart open and made several notes.

Bill grinned. "Let's hope not. If it was that way, I'd never get in up there."

"Well," Michael said, as he clapped his friend on the back. "You go back and tell Marge you aren't going to have to worry about angels for a while, anyway. From what I could hear, your heart sounds fine."

"I'm going to let Marge pay the bill for this," Bill said, chuckling.

"You do that," Michael smiled as he scribbled the charge on the business form and handed it to his receptionist.

"No matter what's wrong with this old body," Bill said. "I always feel a little bit better after you've checked it over."

"Bill—wait—" All at once, he knew what he had to do about Jennie.

No matter what's wrong with this old body, I always feel a little bit better after you've checked it over.

Bill's words had just given it to him right between the eyes. *Bill trusts me. I know what to do to show Jennie I trust her this way, too.*

He had been praying about it for days, just the way he'd promised Dr. Phillips he would. And he couldn't erase the nudging in his spirit now, telling him exactly the right thing to do.

"What can I do for you, Doc?"

"I've got a favor to ask. A big one."

"I'm good at favors," Bill told him. "What is it?"

"Can I borrow your horses? Dan and Kimbo? I'd like to take somebody riding."

"Your boy?"

"No. My—a friend."

Bill raised his eyebrows. "A *woman* friend?"

"You might say that."

"You takin' my advice, Doc? You going out and lookin' for a good woman to take care of you when you get old?"

Michael laughed and nodded his head. "You might say that, too."

"You've got those horses any time you want them. You can borrow the rabbits, too, if you think they'll impress her. And I've been thinking about getting one of those potbellied pigs."

Michael's grin broadened. "No potbellied pigs or rabbits. All I want is the horses for one afternoon. I'll call you and set it up. You tell Marge this office visit is on me. No charge."

"No charge?" Bill practically guffawed. "You mean you aren't gonna send me a bill later?"

"Nope. You're free and clear. Use the money and take Marge on a date."

"That's the best idea you've had all day," Bill said, pulling on his battered tweed hat and shaking Michael's hand. "I'll do that."

Art Sanderson studied the sports page with the trained eye of a perfectionist, making certain the layout looked clean, that none of the headlines bumped together, and that everything made sense.

With his red pencil, he circled two things. One, a headline that bumped against another one so it looked as if it read: "Local runner takes first in 100 mph plunge off hillside."

The second item he circled was a small box on the third page. "Swim team for special kids makes waves with water therapy." He was glad to see they were already running promotional articles for the fund-raiser. He wanted this group to have good play in his pages. The article should have been given better placement. He wanted Jennie's stuff closer to page one. He'd talk with his layout staff about both this afternoon.

He picked up the phone and called Jennie. When she answered the telephone, he could tell something was wrong. She sounded subdued, not like herself at all.

"How are the fund-raiser plans going?" he asked.

"Going really well. I've got several celebrities but I need more."

"You ought to sound more excited about it than you do."

"I've had a thousand things on my mind. The fundraiser's been on the back burner during these past few days—" she paused, knowing full well that the best thing for her mental fatigue right now would be to jump headfirst into this project "—but it's coming along. I need two more famous people and I'll have it."

"Jennie. Are you okay? You don't sound like yourself. Maybe you need to come back to work."

She had to smile. Subtlety was not Art's strong suit. But when she spoke, her words were serious. "Cody's having a tough time at therapy. He's reached his breaking point, I think." He had reached a plateau and had started acting sullen and distant. "He was doing so well for a while that he got all our hopes up."

"Jennie," Art said suddenly. "Do you know anything about Buddy Draper?"

She gave a little start and then grinned. "The Dallas Burn's new coach?" She knew a good deal about Buddy that other people *didn't* know.

"What do you think about getting him involved in this project? I'm betting he'd do it," Art commented. "Considering what he went through himself. You know. Special kids fighting to be winners. Buddy Draper fighting to be a winner. That sort of thing."

It fits right into place. Jennie put a hand on her

heart. Why hadn't she thought of it? It seemed like more and more pieces of her life were fitting together, now that she'd started going to a small group study at Andy's church, now that she'd asked everyone to pray with her so she could trust God more, so she could ask Jesus into her heart.

Andy was going to kill her. But fairy tales came true all the time. *So,* Jennie asked herself, *what are good friends for? To give fairy tales a little push start.*

"I like it, Art," she told him, trying to sound composed and professional when what she really wanted to do was jump up and down. "I'll let you know when I get something put together with him."

She hung up the phone, buoyed once again by the plans for the show, and carried Lester the cat back to see Cody. "Hi, Bear," she said gently, her eyes sparkling as she laid the purring cat in his lap. "What are you doing?"

"Sitting around," he said. He didn't even look at her.

"Darling," she said, kneeling down beside him. "I don't know what to say or do to make it better."

"There isn't anything."

"I've got some great ideas for the swim team fundraiser today. Let's work together. Why don't you come in here and do your book report while I make phone calls?"

He'd started back at school just two days before, not to his old school but to a special school in Plano. The teachers there helped kids who had been out of school for a while to catch up with their studies. "Has something happened at school? Are you wishing you were back in Mrs. Bounds's class?"

"No," he said, shaking his head. His nose started to turn red and she knew he was about to cry again. "I don't miss my friends. I talk to Taylor all the time."

It was time to take a different tack. This gentle pleading hadn't worked with him at all. "I'm tired of the way you're acting, Cody," she told him, standing up abruptly. He started at the change in her voice.

"I'm acting fine," he retorted.

"No, you're not. You're making *me* feel bad because you won't *try*. Well, I refuse to feel bad anymore, young man. You aren't being fair to yourself or to me. You just think about it. You sit there and figure out what's so wrong you have to give up. Then you figure out how to tell me, Cody. Because that's what you're going to have to do before anything gets any better around here."

She turned on her heels and left him sitting there in his wheelchair, with Lester the cat still purring in his lap.

•

"You should do it," Marshall Townsend told Buddy as he stepped out of the shower in the locker room and toweled himself off. "This swim team sounds like a great cause to support."

"They should have asked *you*," Buddy replied. "You're the star player these days." But there was more to it than Marshall knew. Much more. They were talking about Mark *Kendall's* swim team.

At first, when Jennie Stratton had phoned him this morning, he'd actually wondered if Andy had engineered the whole thing. But he'd quickly realized Andy wasn't involved. And suddenly he'd found himself wishing that she was.

"I just don't know if I have the time, Ms. Stratton," he'd told her. "I'm honored to be asked. I'm honored to be included with a list of guests this impressive. I know the swim team is a worthy group. I've heard Mark Kendall works wonders."

"I just don't know if I want any more media attention," Buddy told Marshall now, trying to cover for himself. "Things have finally started dying down."

"Don't tell me you've gotten tired of media attention," Marshall said wryly, running the towel wildly over his head. "You've always thrived on it."

"Nah. Not so much anymore."

Somebody hollered at him from the front office and told him Jennie was on the phone for him again.

"What did you decide?" she asked him.

"I haven't decided anything," he told her pointedly. "You told me you'd give me some time to think about this."

"I'm calling again to convince you that you have to do this, Mr. Draper," she said, the excitement in her voice beginning to wash over him, too. "My editor at the *Times-Sentinel* has just given me permission to do a series of cartoons to promote the event. And I'd love to do one of you—flattering, of course—" she added, laughing. "We'll have cameo appearances from all the other celebrities. But you're the perfect person to be our master of ceremonies for the show."

"You're sure about that."

"I wouldn't be bothering you like this if I wasn't."

He wanted to consider it. But what would happen between him and Andy at this posh media event?

"Well, you've talked me into it. I'll be there," he said, as Marshall walked into the front office and shot him an A-okay sign. "Let me know when you'll need me."

"I'll send you a script and a list of the acts," she told him gleefully. "You don't need to follow the script, though. You can ad-lib all you want to. It'll be fine with us."

"Ad-libbing?" he asked, chuckling and wondering about Andy again. "You'd better watch me close if you're going to let me ad-lib. Or else I'll probably get myself into lots of trouble."

Chapter Seventeen

The next morning just after the little van had come to pick Cody up for school, a pickup truck pulling a horse trailer pulled up to the curb and stopped. Jennie heard the commotion and she peered out through the lace curtains to see who it was. Out stepped Michael clad in faded jeans and an old blue flannel shirt she knew he'd had forever. He looked so handsome and so familiar. She opened the door without giving him a chance to knock.

"Hi," he said. "I knew you'd be home. I tried to call but the phone was busy."

"I've been working on the show for the swim team." She stood staring at him, not inviting him in.

"Can I come in?" he asked finally.

The awkward moment went on a bit too long. "Oh, do." She stepped back and he entered and, as he stepped onto the carpet, she noticed the gray antelope boots he was wearing. "You make a good cowboy."

"Yeah," he said, grinning. "All I need's the hat."

"Everything's coming together for the fund-raiser. It's going to be quite a production. Mark's already got the kids practicing, too."

"I think you should work on the fund-raiser tomorrow. I've got two horses out there—" here he put on his best cowboy swagger and voice "—that are just hankerin' to take you for a ride across the blacklands of North Texas."

"Oh, no!" She started to giggle. "You're crazy. You know that?"

"I have something important to talk to you about. Get into your jeans. We're going for a ride."

"Michael."

He saw all her doubts on her face. "Come on, Jennie. The horses are all loaded up and waiting. Don't turn me down now."

She considered. "I've got to get back by four-fifteen. That's when the van brings Cody back from school."

"That's fine. We've got all day. We'll beat the traffic back into town."

Jennie changed quickly and rejoined him downstairs, her heart thumping like a schoolgirl's all over again.

"These are Bill Josephs's horses," he told her as they climbed into the truck. "You remember him? He's been my patient a long time. They used to have a ranch over on Preston Road. Now they have a little place out past Mesquite."

"I do remember him. His wife's name is Marge?"

"That's him. They don't use the horses much anymore. He said he'd love for us to take them out and give them some exercise."

"So…where are we going?"

"You'll see."

"We need to make plans for Cody to come to your place," she said in an effort to fill the silence. "You want me to bring him over on Sunday?"

"Let's talk about that later."

He just kept driving. He drove them far north of Plano to a pretty house atop a knoll that had acres and acres of land and a perfect white fence lining the driveway. Down past the house on the other side of the drive stood the corrals. He backed the trailer in and climbed out to unload the horses.

"This place is beautiful," she said, climbing out of the truck and crossing her arms over her pretty blue sweater. "Are the owners patients of yours, too?"

He shook his head. "Nope. Just somebody I know." That was all he intended to say for now.

She stepped over to the side of the knoll and looked across the pasture that was just now beginning to tinge with the green of early springtime. "You can see for miles."

He came to stand beside her, leading a horse. "That's pretty much what Texas is known for, away from the city."

She turned to him, only a breath away, her skin as soft and pink in the cool morning air as the embroidered roses on her sweater. It was everything he could do to keep from kissing her. But he wasn't going to do that, not while he still had so much to tell her.

He handed her the reins to Bill Josephs's chestnut mare and he lifted her easily so she could mount. She kept the horse still, waiting for him, while he led the other horse, a dun, out of the trailer. But he waved her on. "Go ahead, Jen. I'll catch up with you."

"You don't mind?"

He shook his head.

She kicked the horse and they were on their way. "See you in the pasture!"

Michael watched them both for a moment, smiling at the two bouncing ponytails as they disappeared just over the knoll. He saddled up his own horse and hurried to catch up. "Hey, you!" he called as he galloped up beside her. "I didn't know you were going to ride across half the county!"

"This feels wonderful," she called back, laughing. Her wheat yellow hair was streaming back behind her and she had tears running down her cheeks from the wind. "I know it sounds wild," she told him. "But I feel so *free* right now. After everything that's been weighing heavy on my life for so long."

They rode along together in silence. It was one of those precious days when the black earth and the tender sprouts of grass poking up through the brown smelled herbal and rich and full of promise.

"What are the horses' names? Did Bill tell you?"

"He told me," Michael answered her, smiling. "He treats these horses like they're his children. Your horse is Kimbo. Mine is Dan."

"Cody would like to ride sometime. Do you think Bill would let him?"

"Bill's been suggesting it." Michael chuckled. "Bill has a lot of suggestions."

She tilted her head at him and grinned. He loved watching her. She looked like one of the little sparrows that kept twittering and rising from the pecan trees around them. "Dan is a pretty common name, but I wonder where he got 'Kimbo.'"

"I think he named her after his daughter."

She laughed. "An honor, I'm sure." She laid long, slender fingers against the horse's neck. "You're a good girl, Kimbo. A fine horse."

They rode farther, neither speaking.

"You want to race?" Michael suggested.

"Do you know something I don't know?" she asked him. "Which one of these horses is faster?"

"I have no idea. That's why I wanted to race. We could find out."

She leaned low over the chestnut's neck. "Okay. You're on." Before he knew what was happening, she was galloping ahead of him like a Kentucky Derby jockey and the distance was spreading.

"Hey!" he hollered. "I didn't say 'go!'"

"No," she shouted back, pulling even farther ahead. "I did."

He spurred Dan and the horse leapt forward. Michael felt as if he were flying as he pounded after her. The distance began to close. Up ahead, he could hear Jennie laughing and urging Kimbo on. "Come on, boy," he whispered. "Let's get her."

Dirt flew up in clouds from Kimbo's racing hooves. Jennie's ponytail was long gone. Her hair flew out from her head like a banner.

He'd just about caught up with her. They raced together across the field toward an unknown goal, running just for the joy of running, the horses flank to flank, the sweat pouring from beneath their saddle blankets despite the cool day.

Dan inched up now, slowly, slowly, until his nose bobbed up and down directly beside the horse he challenged. And then, at long last, the nose went past and the race was over. "I won! I won!" Michael shouted as he pulled up. He winked at her. "That was the finish line back there."

"No," she said in her soft Texas drawl. "There wasn't a finish line. I just wanted to see how far I could go before you won."

"Ha!" he said, throwing his head back and wiping sweat off his face with a shirtsleeve.

"We got pretty far," she added, grinning.

"Thank you," he said. "For letting me win."

"Thank you," she said. "For the race."

"There's a creek up ahead. We probably ought to let these guys rest and have a drink."

"Sounds fine to me," she said. "You know the lay of this land pretty well, Michael."

"I've walked it several times."

They came toward the creek. The horses began to nicker as soon as they saw the water. Michael and Jennie loosened the reins and the horses lowered their heads. Dan and Kimbo snorted and sucked water with such relish it made Michael smile. "Sounds like a herd of elephants drinking here instead of two horses."

"We ran them pretty hard." But she didn't really participate in the joke. Her mind was somewhere else.

Jennie's senses were suddenly filled with her ex-husband, filled with the nearness of him, with the warm gamy smell of the horses, the creaking of worn leather.

She reached across and touched his hand where his fingers lay open atop the knotted reins.

He turned to face her. "They've had enough to drink, I think," he said quietly. "We'd best get them out of this creek."

He turned his horse back toward the house and Jennie followed him, seeing how serious he was, hoping she hadn't done anything wrong. They'd ridden without saying anything for what seemed like forever before he turned to her. It was time he told her what he'd brought her here to say. "There's something I've been praying about, Jen. In my heart of hearts, I feel it's what my Heavenly Father wants me to do."

"What?"

"I'm letting go. I'm letting go of everything."

"What do you mean?"

"I'm giving you full custody of Cody, Jen."

Shock silenced her.

"My lawyers have been working on it. All they need is your signature."

Jennie stared at him, stunned. She pulled the horse to a full stop. "After everything you fought for, Michael? Why? Why now?"

"Jen," he said, stopping Dan just beside her. "I've watched you give Cody everything you had to give him."

With tears in her eyes, she nodded.

"It's what I know I have to do. I don't want him to have to go back and forth between us. I want him to have one home, one life, where he belongs."

"Until he's stronger?"

"No. Until forever. In a home where he belongs."

"But…Cody…" It was all she could say. She reeled from the enormity of his sacrifice.

"It's too hard for him to keep going back and forth. I'll be in his life as much as I always have. But this will give him the strength to keep doing what he needs to do."

The tears began to course down her face. Michael grieved, too, but he didn't regret what he was doing.

This is what love is, he thought. *This is what God had showed him.* Love, different in countless ways from what he and Jennie had shared before. Love, free from suspicion and guilt and jealousy. Not romance but love, tempered to strength on the anvil of what they'd been through—a broken marriage—a son's illness—a binding faith.

"I'm afraid," she told him quietly.

"Because you'd have him all to yourself?"

Reluctantly, she nodded.

"But you won't be by yourself," he said, his own tears threatening again. "I'll be there, too. I'll always be there for you and Cody. Remember that."

This time, it was Michael's turn to reach across the horse and touch Jennie's hand.

"Michael," she said. "I don't know what to say."

"You don't have to say anything."

She gripped his hand, held on to it as tightly as she wanted to hang on to him.

Gently, tenderly, he lifted her hand, their fingers intertwined, until the back of her hand rested against the cool skin of his cheek.

Chapter Eighteen

Andy cleared out all the equipment from the gym at Children's one morning, leaving only the tumbling pads and parallel bars, which she placed in the center of the room. Jennie drove Cody to the hospital and Michael met them there. Michael and Jennie watched anxiously as Andy and an assistant lifted their son from the wheelchair, one of his little arms wrapped around each of their shoulders, and maneuvered him toward the equipment.

"Here you go, kiddo," Andy told him as she helped him circle his fingers around each bar. "This is it. Time to stand up and show all of us what you're made of!"

"I'm a kid," Cody told Andy. "You know what I'm made of. Skin and stuff."

"More than that," Andy shot back at him. "I've seen you work." She nodded at the assistant and the man took on the full brunt of Cody's weight. Andy stepped out between the bars in front of him. "Now. It's time. Let's see you straighten those legs and put some muscles to use. There you go. Ease it down. Think about what you're doing."

Cody's eyes locked with Andy's. Jennie held her breath. Michael's mouth moved in prayer. Cody's legs buckled beneath him and he began to sink. Andy caught him and helped pull him back up.

"No," Andy said. "Not like that. Think strong. Think legs of steel. Decide you're a robot, like C3P0 on *Star Wars,* and you've got to lock your knees and raise yourself as tall as you can."

"C3P0's a *droid*," Cody argued, obviously trying to keep everyone's mind off the task at hand.

"Whatever he was," Andy shot back. "He stood strong and tall and helped Luke Skywalker."

Andy nodded at the assistant again.

He relinquished his grip on Cody a second time.

"Now, Cody," Andy urged. *"Now."*

Beside the door, Michael gripped Jennie's hand in his own.

"Please, Cody," Jennie murmured. "Please try."

"Come on, son," Michael chimed in. "I *know* you can do it."

Cody's knees turned inward…outward…one outward and one inward again…and the little boy's posture started to crumple. Again the assistant rescued him.

"That was better," Andy encouraged him. "You

balanced a little bit longer." She knew she had to encourage him. Cody had one more chance. If he couldn't do this, she wouldn't do much more with him today. They were all expecting an awful lot of him. It was best if they didn't tire him out. "I want to see you try it one more time."

"I don't want to try again," he said, whining.

"I remember when you used to try everything. You do this and you'll be back on the right track, kiddo. You just wait and see. You'll be *so glad* if you try."

This time, Andy's words seemed to spark something within Cody. He shook his head and squared his shoulders and sighed as he tried again.

"That's it…" Andy egged him on. "Come on…come on…"

Michael clenched Jennie's hand so fiercely she scarcely had feeling in it anymore. She gritted her teeth and held her breath as she silently prayed for Cody.

"You can do it, Cody," Andy whispered to him. "I'm proud of you! I see you trying! I know you can!"

For one instant…maybe less than an instant…it seemed that Cody was bearing the brunt of his own weight. His legs wobbled…once…twice…and he lost his balance. He began to topple. The assistant moved to grab him but he missed.

"Ooof," Cody grunted when he hit the ground. And, as Michael and Jennie ran to him and Andy lifted him up, Cody began to cry in earnest.

"I hate this!" he bawled as tears of frustration

streamed down his cheeks. "I hate my legs. I hate my head. I hate having to *fight* to make things work right. I hate this." He started pounding the mats with his hands. "I—hate—this!"

"Cody, son," Michael said, reaching out to him. "Your mother and I—we hate it, too. But you've got to keep fighting to stand, to get well."

But Cody would hear none of it. "I don't care what you and Mom think. I don't care what you and Mom do!" he shouted. "You two are the dumbest parents alive. You don't even understand."

Michael felt his anger rising. He did his best to keep it in check. "You watch yourself, young man. I don't want to hear that tone of voice from you again."

"You aren't being fair!" Cody shouted at him. "You and Mom aren't being fair!"

Jennie knelt beside them both. "Cody. We want to understand you and help you with everything you're going through. But you've got to try to help us."

A new flood of tears began. "That's just it, Mom! That's always it! All you tell me anymore is try. Try, try, try—I'm sick of trying."

"That's because we know what's best for you," they said together, precisely in unison. It would have been funny if Cody hadn't been so upset.

"You tell me to fight all the time and to *try* and wish for one thing and you tell me not to fight and to wish for another," he cried at them. "All the time I can see that it's you and Dad who aren't trying...."

At his words, Jennie's face went ashen. And here, Cody buckled his knees up beneath him—a very promising movement as Andy saw it—buried his face against his legs, and continued to wail. "It's you who won't try. It's you. And it's Dad. So if you two won't try to be together again, I'm not going to try, either."

Andy sat beside him, holding him as he hollered with frustration. But there was nothing she could do. At last Cody was voicing his frustration.

"Oh, Cody," Jennie whispered, devastated. "Is that it, then? But it's such a different kind of trying."

"It doesn't matter, Mom," Cody told her. "It doesn't matter that it's different. Because it's what I want more than anything else in the whole world."

On the afternoon of the fund-raiser, Andy stood backstage at the gigantic pavilion where the show would be held, directing five little girls from Mark's team and putting the finishing touches on a routine Jennie had suggested. They were doing a funny skit in which they all wore bright yellow leotards and danced with soccer balls.

The show was only hours away. The *Times-Sentinel* had yet to announce who the master of ceremonies would be. The newspaper had billed him all week as a "local celebrity" and a "must-see attraction." Even Jennie was keeping it a secret.

"We decided that would be part of the fun," she explained when Andy questioned her for what seemed like the ninety-ninth time. "Everybody will come to see who the mystery celebrity is. I guarantee they won't be disappointed." She shook her head and gave Andy a little grin. "*You* won't be disappointed, either."

Now, as Andy worked on the dance with the kids, she pushed a bright red headband up over her bangs, readjusted her own black leotard and motioned for them all to follow her. "Vanessa. When you kick, turn just like this, okay?" She couldn't tell them to point their toes. They hadn't yet mastered that skill. "Now. Let's try it again. One—two—"

Just as the music began, one little girl lost control of her soccer ball. It rolled across the stage before anyone could grab it, and it disappeared into the wings.

"Oops!" Andy stopped the routine and ran to get it. "Hang on, you guys," she said, laughing as she fumbled around in the dark. "We can't go on without our props."

Suddenly, a big hand reached out of the darkness and handed the ball to her. "Is this what you're looking for?"

"Yes." The ball rolled into her arms and she clasped it to her chest. Her eyes tried to focus in the darkness.

"Didn't know there would be soccer balls in the show tonight," he commented offhandedly. "Must have something to do with the master of ceremonies."

Andy's eyes adjusted. She caught her breath.

"Buddy?"

She couldn't believe he was standing there, this close, chuckling and talking to her.

"Buddy." She said his name again just to convince herself he was real. "*What* are you doing here?"

"This is where they told me to come. I'm in the right place, aren't I? For the swim team fund-raiser?"

"You're coming to the show? Then you're supposed to be in the audience." Her heart was pounding and she couldn't think. "And you're early. It doesn't start for another hour."

He chuckled again, a warm, melodious laugh that brought back a thousand memories. "No. I'm not early. I'm *in* the show."

"You're *in* the show?"

"Yeah. Is that okay? Are you going to kick me out? No pun intended." As he eyed the soccer ball again.

She still couldn't believe it. At that moment Jennie walked up to them. "Oh, good, Buddy. Here you are. I've been waiting for you. Do you have any more questions about the script?"

"One or two things." They talked briefly. Jennie answered his questions and told him when to introduce everyone and in what order. "We're opening the show with the soccer ball routine," Jennie said, glancing at Andy for the first time, as if Buddy's presence meant nothing to either of them.

When she caught the glint in Andy's eyes, she grinned back, hoping Andy wasn't making plans to strangle her.

But from the way Buddy kept glancing away from the script and gazing at Andy, Jennie was willing to bet things were going according to plan. "At the end of the routine, Buddy will run out on stage and we'll introduce him. That's how everybody will find out that Buddy Draper is our 'mystery master of ceremonies.'"

"Even me?" Andy asked her pointedly. "Is that how I'm supposed to find out, too?"

"No. Of course not you," Jennie said, laughing. "Because you've found it out now."

But Andy didn't even hear that last remark. She was looking at Buddy and he was looking at her as if they were the only two people left in the world.

"You let Jennie talk you into this," Andy said, half accusing him, half teasing him, after her friend had walked away.

"More or less. But I thought it was a good idea, too."

"You—"

"Yeah," Buddy said. "Me. You remember. The one who's a coward. The one you never wanted to see again. Well, tough luck, sweetheart," he drawled in his best Bogart imitation.

"Show time! Thirty minutes!" somebody shouted. And, all around them, lights began to come on and the girls in little yellow leotards started to jump up and down. "Come on! We've got to finish our dance or we won't remember how to do it at all!"

"I've got to go." She clutched the ball tighter and

gave him a sad little smile. "I'm sorry for so many things, Buddy. I was wrong to think I knew what God's calling on your life was. I should have been willing to stand beside you on the journey." Then, "Good luck."

But he touched her arm before she could turn away. "This has nothing to do with luck, you know. It took a lot of fighting. And, looking at you, I don't believe I'm finished. Fighting, I mean. For what I want."

Out in the audience, at five minutes before seven, select members of the Dallas Symphony struck up a rousing rendition of a calypso song and the lights began to fade. "I've gotta go, Dad!" Cody told Michael. "They told me I had to go backstage when the music started."

"You'd better get back there then. I'll be watching you."

"I'm in the second song. I'll be the third one on the right." It would be his only appearance in the show. He just hadn't been ready to try some of the harder numbers. "Be sure you find me. In the first song, be sure to find Megan and Vanessa. Mom will point them out to you. They're on my swim team, too."

"I'll show him," Jennie promised. "Now get back there. Andy's going to kill me already. I don't want you to hold up the show."

Michael and Jennie watched as he wheeled his wheelchair up the front aisle away from them. He turned and waved once just before he started up the ramp to go backstage. "Don't forget to watch me, Dad!"

"I won't!" Michael called back. "I promise."

After Cody left, Jennie squeezed Michael's hand. "He's so proud and excited."

"I know," Michael said softly. "It's terrific to see him happy and enthusiastic again the way he's been this week." He squeezed her hand back. "It's amazing how it helps to get something off your chest."

"I know that." They sat together in the front row, not quite so afraid to be beside one another any longer. "He's done so well at the rehearsals because he knew we'd be here together."

Really, Jennie should have been backstage with Art and Andy and Buddy running the show. But everything had been practiced and polished what seemed like a hundred times over. Art was pleased with the newspaper's involvement and he was taking full advantage of it. He'd requested specifically that he be the one to introduce the mayor. It was easy for him to cue Buddy, too. So, despite all the work she'd done, there was really nothing more Jennie could do than sit beside Michael, two proud parents side by side in the front row, as the lights faded to total darkness, and Art Sanderson stepped out on stage.

"Ladies and gentlemen," Art said, the lights glinting on his gray hair. He spread his arms wide, looking spectacular in the black tuxedo and bright red cummerbund they'd rented for him. "The *Dallas Times-Sentinel* and the North Dallas Swim Dream Team want to welcome you to a spectacular evening, an evening of frolic and special guests...."

She leaned over and whispered to Michael. "The swim team's never had a name before. They had to come up with something so they could welcome everybody like this."

She was thrilled by the turnout. Several large corporations, one major downtown bank and several well-heeled individuals had supported the event. She'd seen Harv Siskell and Marshall Townsend take seats not ten minutes before.

Suddenly the spotlight wheeled around toward Jennie and, before she knew what was happening, the light was shining right in her face. Art was saying, "Ms. Jennie Stratton. A woman with foresight and guts, a woman with the know-how and the audacity to think a dream like this one could actually come true."

Strange, she didn't feel like a woman with foresight and guts, a woman who thought dreams could come true. She only felt herself like someone who had been led on a journey...someone who had been wooed... someone who God loved.

With this new certainty in her heart, she felt as if everything...everything...was possible.

"Jennie," Art said from the podium. "Stand up so we can show you our appreciation."

She did as told, waving at the crowd as the hall filled with thunderous applause. As she sat down, the music began to swell again and Art bid his farewell. It was time for the show to begin.

The curtain rose to Andy's seven dancers, all clad in sunny yellow leotards and grappling with the black-and-white leather balls, spinning them this way and that, behind a huge piece of green-blue cellophane that made it look as if they were dancing underwater. "Buddy's coming out at the end of this one," she leaned over and whispered to Michael. "Then after Buddy talks a while, it'll be Cody's turn...."

"Shh," Michael said, leaning toward her and grinning, then unable to ignore the urge to kiss her on the nose. She was so enthusiastic, almost childlike. She reminded him of the way she'd been years ago when they first met. Yet, beneath it all, he knew there was something more, something different, something strong about her now. She'd grown up during the past months and so had he. "Don't tell me any more. This is all supposed to be a surprise, remember?"

She covered her mouth with her hand and looked apologetic. "Sorry! I forgot. I really forgot. I'm just so excited about it all."

He draped one arm around her shoulder and snuggled close to enjoy the performance. And, at that moment, his pager went off.

It sounded loud enough to make people around them notice. He turned to Jennie, knowing how upset she would be.

"I have to call the hospital," he told her. "I'll go outside and use my cell. Maybe I can get somebody to stand in for me."

"Oh, Michael. See if you can."

He rushed out to use his phone. When he came back moments later, his face was pale. "I have to go. It's Bill Josephs. He's gone into cardiac arrest and they're bringing him in."

On stage, Buddy Draper ran out amid the girls' bouncing soccer balls and, around them, everyone was applauding again. Buddy was going to be the hit of the night.

"Ladies and gentlemen!" a voice from nowhere shouted out over the sound system. "Coach of the Dallas Burn, Mr. Buddy Draper!"

Cody's number was the very next one.

"Jennie," he said, taking both of her shoulders in his firm grip, desperate to make her understand. "If I had any choice—any choice at all—I would stay with you. You are the most important thing in the world to me." Gently, ever so briefly, he touched her lips. "I never want you to question that again."

She nodded, not saying anything, tears streaming down her face, tears she never bothered to hide or wipe away.

Chapter Nineteen

With a chilled heart, Michael raced toward the emergency room at Parkland Hospital where they'd brought Bill.

As he ran toward E.R.'s cardiac room two, Michael saw Marge in the waiting room. With overflowing eyes and a streaming nose, she told him she'd asked for him immediately when the ambulance arrived to pick them up.

"You did the right thing," he told her now as he squeezed her tightly and handed her a handkerchief. "Dr. Rosenstein's one of the best in Dallas. And I'm going to do my best for him now, too."

"You do that," she said, her voice still wavering as she released him.

Within seconds Michael was beside Bill and getting the rundown from Rosenstein. "What's been done, Mitch?"

"Patient found at home by spouse," Rosenstein told him. "Time of collapse unknown, approximately ten minutes. EMTs started resuscitation en route. First rhythm transmitted was V-fib. No blood pressure en route."

They'd gotten Bill in quickly but Marge had been on the telephone talking to their daughter when it happened. She hadn't heard him cry out. No one knew exactly how long he'd been unconscious before she found him. Add that to the time it took to get the ambulance out to their farm and back.

"Patient was defibbed times three," Rosenstein continued. "An amp of Epi was given. Patient then received into the E.R., was defibbed again. Pushed Lidocaine, 85 milligrams. As you can see—" Mitch Rosenstein gestured toward the monitor and at the eight other people in the room working frantically "—still no response."

"Fine," Michael told him. "I'll take over, Mitch." He stood only feet away from his friend, a man he felt he had known forever. He knew he couldn't make emotional judgments now, yet he had to make the correct decisions and make them without feeling. "Defib with 360 joules."

"All clear," the paramedic warned.

The jolt of electricity lifted Bill's body clear up off the table. Michael checked the monitor. Still no response. The steady hum of the machine continued mercilessly. Michael felt as if it were shouting at him.

"Come on, Bill," he whispered as nurses and paramedics and EMTs performed their duties in a frenzy around him. "Come on." *Father, help him. We don't want to let him go yet.*

He had a decision to make. He gave the command loudly. "Administer Lidocaine, 43 milligrams."

A nurse ran to carry out his orders. He checked the clock on the wall. Time was of the essence. He looked at the monitor, waiting for a certain sign, anything, that he was getting somewhere.

The monitor hadn't changed. "Defib again," Michael commanded.

"All clear," the paramedic shouted.

Again the jolt. Again the lifting. Again no response on the monitor.

Bill. Come on. You've got a wife who loves you waiting out there.

And a friend who cares about you in here, too, he might have thought. Only he didn't dare. He couldn't equate the motionless man on the stretcher with the man who'd given him a tour of his barn and had constantly chided him about his bills. And, now, it had come to this.

Michael was getting desperate. "Give him Bertylium, 425 milligrams."

The line on the monitor continued. The evidence of any heart impulses was growing fainter.

"Defib."

"All clear."

No response.

"Let's go with more Epi."

No response.

"Defib again."

"All clear," the paramedic repeated.

No response.

"I want double the Bertylium. 850 milligrams this time."

The monitor continued to hum ominously. He didn't even have to look up and check it this time. He knew what it was going to tell him.

"Defib again." It seemed to go on forever, these electrical jolts and all of his choices of magic medicine.

One of the nurses was keeping track for him or he'd have no idea now how many times they'd gone back and forth trying to save his patient. He did everything by the book, alternating between Atropine and Epinephrine, feeling as if hours had gone by while he sweated as though he were running a marathon.

"Bill," he said aloud. "Hang in there, Bill. You've got to."

"Michael," Mitch Rosenstein said from behind him. "You've got to think about calling the code."

"I know that, Mitch," he said calmly. "I'm not ready to do that yet." Louder. "Defib again."

"All clear," said the paramedic.

"Come—on—Bill," Michael whispered from between gritted teeth.

A jolt. Bill's torso practically went flying off the table.

Another buzzer sounded. The line on the monitor

had gone totally straight. "Doctor," the EMT said. "We have asystole." No heart response at all.

Father, no, Michael thought. *I've lost him.*

"Administer Epi," he ordered frantically. But in his heart of hearts, he knew it was over. He'd done the best he could do. And it hadn't been good enough. After everything, he still had no response.

"What's our pressure?" he asked futilely.

"We have no BP."

"I'm going to try one more time," he told them all. And after that, he knew he had to stop. He owed it to Bill to stop. "Defib again."

"All clear."

To Michael, the very last time seemed as if it happened in slow motion, the nurses clearing away, the EMT climbing off the stool away from Bill's chest, the electrical jolt surging through the man on the table. But, again, nothing happened. *Father, all this letting go. I give him over to Your hands.*

He said almost beneath his breath. "Let's call it."

No one stirred.

He hadn't said it loudly enough. "What did you say, Dr. Stratton?" someone asked him.

"I said—" this time his voice was clear and firm and loud "—let's call it."

The frenzy had ended. Nurses silently went about turning the machines off one by one.

"You did a good job, Doctor," Mitch Rosenstein said. "You did everything you could do and then some. I'll write that in my report."

"Thanks," Michael should have said. He should have thanked his colleague for his help. They both should have said, "Sorry, better luck next time—there's always a next time, you know—" But he couldn't do it. He'd just lost one of his dearest friends. He felt as though he'd lost a member of his family, as well.

He thought of Marge still in the waiting room, still pacing alone, still praying and hoping it might not be over. "I'll tell his wife," Michael said.

"Fine," Rosenstein agreed sadly.

But when Michael took his first step out of the cardiac room and saw the lovely, elderly woman waiting for him, it took everything he could muster to keep from breaking down.

"Doc? Michael?" she asked in a timid voice. But she didn't have to ask. She saw his face and the tears in his eyes.

"Marge." He reached for her, taking one of her wrinkled hands in his own and holding it there. "I did everything I could. And Bill was strong. But this was a massive heart attack. It was just too much for him."

Tears came to her eyes now, too. "He's gone, isn't he?"

Michael nodded.

He watched helplessly as her composure crumpled

and she buried her face in his chest, her body racked with sorrow.

Michael wrapped his arms around her, and held her as the nurses and all the assistants started coming out of the cardiac room to get out of their scrubs. They each cast knowing eyes in his direction.

They didn't know the half of it. As he gently held the old woman he'd known for what seemed like forever, as he watched her begin to come to grips with the fact she'd have to live her life now without her husband, he came to grips with the fact that he'd have to live his life without Jennie now, too.

He had betrayed her, left her alone to be there for Cody when she'd needed him most. It would be months, years, perhaps a lifetime, before he forgot the anguished acceptance he'd seen in her eyes.

And so, he thought, *it's over for us, too.*

No, you crazy fool, he reminded himself. *It was all over four years ago in a divorce court.*

Marge choked back the sobs against his chest and did her best to compose herself. "Michael. I'm so sorry."

"Oh, Marge," he said, gripping her tighter, his own eyes still bright with his pain. "Don't apologize, please. Go ahead and *cry…*"

"I know that you both did everything you knew to do. I thank you for that."

"I wouldn't have done less for him."

She was obviously in shock, and her mind was going

in a thousand different directions at once. "Do you want the horses?" she asked. "I can't keep them by myself. He'd love for you to have Dan and Kimbo." She started to cry again, realizing she'd spoken of him as if he was still here. She gazed up at him with eyes so full of despair she looked as if a part of her own soul had died, too. And, really, Michael supposed it had. "I don't know—what—to—do now."

"Is there anyone I can call for you, Marge?"

She shook her head. "My daughter and her husband are on their way. They would have been here sooner but the kids were in bed and they had to find a sitter. And now they don't know he's *gone...*"

Michael lowered Marge Josephs to the sofa in the waiting room and held her there until her family came. After that, he finally slipped away to grieve alone. It had been a torturous night.

"Everybody ready backstage for the second number!" Andy shouted.

"We're going to get a hot fudge sundae after the show," Cody told Andy. "My dad promised. You want to come with us?"

"Thanks for inviting me, little one," Andy told him. "I can't make it tonight. I'll tell your dad to get you an extra scoop so you can eat mine, too." She squeezed him. He'd been trying hard again lately and she was proud of him. "After how hard you've worked to get ready for this show the past two weeks, you deserve six hot fudge sundaes."

"Yum! You better tell my dad that. You can find him easy. He's sitting in the front row with Mom."

"You get onstage," she said, giving his chair a little shove. "You're on."

"See ya later, Andy."

"Do good."

Cody rolled out onstage and took his place beside five other kids from the swim team. The music began to play, and in the pit below them Cody could see the conductor leading it, his baton pointing crisply at each new group of instruments as they faded in.

Cody tried to see his mom and dad but he couldn't. The huge spotlight was shining right into his eyes. At least he knew they were there. He could feel them there.

The microphone stuck to his chest was bugging him but he knew he had to keep it right on his collar. They had already practiced this way all afternoon. He knew the little microphone would help everybody hear his lines.

"Down at the corner," he said as loudly as he could, "where the old well stood…"

He finished his poem and they all started singing. Cody puffed out his chest as far as he could. He sang so hard he knew he was red in the face. He stumbled on a couple of the words because he forgot to think when they came up. But that was okay because he knew his mom and dad would see that he was trying his best.

He even forgot to be scared. He just kept singing and smiling. Every so often he peered out through the blinding light, doing his best to find his parents. But he couldn't.

When the song ended, Cody felt as if he was just getting started. He wanted it to go on all night long. Everybody was clapping for them and, one by one, they each took the little bow they'd practiced with Mark.

"Way to go!" Andy shouted from the wings.

Buddy Draper stood right beside her. He was clapping, too. "You nailed it, kid!"

Just as Cody turned his wheelchair to start off stage, the curtain began to come down and the big spotlight flashed off. The audience became people again. He could see heads and hundreds of hands and faces.

"Mom!" he shouted. "Dad! Did you like it?" And then, his breath caught. The only thing beside his mom was an empty chair.

"Where did he go, Mom?" he asked as they hugged in the aisle and Jennie told him what a good job he had done.

She knelt down beside his chair, and touched his hand. "He had to go to the hospital, Bear. One of his patients got sick." She paused. "He didn't want to leave, sweetheart. I saw his face. He wanted to see you so badly."

"The whole time I was singing, I thought he was there."

"I know," she said, touching his little face. "I could tell by the way you were singing. I've never seen anybody sing quite so well." She kissed him. "Come on. Let's go get that hot fudge sundae."

When they got to the restaurant, they both ordered sundaes and, as the waitress brought them out, they giggled at how huge they were. The ice cream was jammed into icy fountain glasses and covered with huge knots of whipped cream. As Cody poured chocolate over his, Jennie tried Michael on his cell phone.

"I'm going to call your father," she told Cody. Then when he didn't answer, she called the main number at the hospital. She waited on the line for almost ten minutes while they paged him. "He must still be in the cardiac room," the nurse told her.

Jennie and Cody finished their sundaes and headed home. Cody went to bed. Every half hour Jennie tried to reach him.

It was past midnight when Jennie found a nurse she knew. Someone told her that Sally Rogers was on the floor. Sally usually worked with Michael when he had patients at Parkland. "Let me talk to her. She'll tell me what I need to know."

"I don't know where he is, Jennie," Sally told her when she came to the phone. "We were all in cardiac room two but nobody's answering over there. Michael hasn't checked out yet. I know he's still in the building."

"What's going on with Bill Josephs? Will he be okay?"

Sally hesitated, but only for a moment. "They lost

him, Jennie. Michael worked on him a long time but he couldn't save him."

Jennie hung up and sat down by the phone, thinking of Michael, remembering his words, *You're the most important thing in the world to me.*

She wasn't going to be influenced by her doubts anymore. God had a hope and a promise for her, and she was going to find it.

Jennie bundled Cody up in blankets and carried him downstairs. She decided to drop him off at Andy's house. She knew she was imposing, but she had to find Michael.

He woke up when she put him in the car. "Where are we going?" he asked, rubbing his eyes.

"No need to wake up," she whispered. "I'm going to take you to Andy's for a while. I'm going to the hospital to be with your dad, okay?"

Even though he was half asleep, he smiled. "Yeah," he said, yawning. "That's real okay."

Jennie found Michael in the hospital chapel. She guessed he might be there quietly grieving for his friend. And, as she silently closed the massive wooden door and stepped up behind him, she knew without a doubt that, because of the fine, caring doctor he was, there were going to be times in their lives that he couldn't put her first.

What mattered was what she'd seen in his eyes when

he'd left the fund-raiser. What mattered were the words he'd shared, how he'd made her feel, how he'd made her trust him.

She wanted to be there for him, now, and for a lifetime.

"Michael," she whispered. "I'm here."

He raised his eyes and looked at her almost as if he didn't recognize her. "Jen?"

"Hi." It was the only thing she could think of to say as she broke out into a crazy grin.

"What are you doing here?"

She reached out to him and stroked one strand of hair back from his face. She tucked it behind his ear. It was exactly the way she would have comforted Cody. "I heard about Bill. I'm so sorry."

Michael nodded his head, still too much in grief and shock to question her presence. "I can't believe we lost him, Jen. I tried everything. I don't remember it ever being so rough...."

"You probably have never done that for someone you cared so much about."

He met her eyes. "You're right."

"I figured things weren't going well when you didn't come back to the show."

"You thought I'd come back?" So he'd betrayed her once and disappointed her twice.

"Only if you could get away. Cody did fine. Very well, in fact."

"I wish I could have seen him." *I wish Bill could have*

lived. I wish we hadn't messed up so long ago. His wish list was a mile long.

"Cody understands."

"He does?"

She nodded. "Yes." Her voice was so soft now he almost couldn't hear her. "Because he loves you very, very much."

He smiled at her, a sad smile but a smile just the same. "That helps me, you know."

"I'm so sorry, Michael." All of a sudden, she was babbling like a child. "I've had no right…I've done this to you all your life. I've been making you choose—or *say* you were choosing—when it really wasn't your choice at all…."

With two hands, he cupped the top of her head and swept her long, straight hair away from her temples so he could read her eyes. "Are you saying that you're forgiving me?"

She shook her head. "I'm saying there isn't anything to forgive. Or there isn't now anyway. Once maybe there would have been. But not anymore. That's changed, hasn't it, Michael?"

"Yes," he said, his voice gentle. "It has." He gazed up at the window. "I can't believe Bill's gone. I had to come out of that cardiac room and tell Marge. Oh, Jen, that's the hardest thing I've ever done, telling her like that. And the only thing I kept thinking was that she'd lost Bill and that I'd lost you. I envied her even as I grieved with her. Because the two of them grew old together and we wouldn't have the chance."

"I'm so proud of you," she said. "Don't you see? It's exactly the same thing we've been telling Cody all these months. You didn't save Bill. But you gave him your best shot. You tried. Hasn't watching Cody all these months taught you the importance of that?" Then she gripped his arms with both hands. "You may have lost Bill Josephs, Michael," she told him. "But you haven't lost us. You haven't lost me and Cody."

He stared at her. "What are you saying? Are you saying you're willing to try again?"

As though the gesture were made by someone else, she felt herself nodding. The next thing she knew, he crushed her in his arms. "I'm saying I don't want to lose you," she said. "I'm saying that I want to save us." She pulled back just a bit from him so she could read his face. "I'm saying that I love you, Michael—very, very much." And she couldn't stop herself from laughing then because she'd finally said it. "All over again."

He thought of letting Bill Josephs go. His good friend was probably telling an angel a joke, right about now, now that he'd arrived in heaven.

Michael thought about the times God had called him to let go. He'd probably have to be reminded of the lesson plenty more times.

But he saw now, how if you let something go to God, sometimes it got returned to you a thousandfold.

He held Jennie's shoulders, still astounded that the heartache of the past few hours was redeeming itself now with such promise. "I love you, Jennie. I don't think I ever stopped loving you—ever—but now it's more. More—and different."

"I know," she said as she nestled against him and felt safer, more complete, than she'd ever felt before. "I know."

All three of them sat on the couch the next night, munching popcorn Michael had made, talking about their lives together and planning the wedding.

"I knew it! I knew it!" Cody cried when they told him. "Are we going to live here? Or are we going to live at Dad's house?"

Michael glanced at Jennie. They hadn't had time to discuss this. But, really, things had happened so fast they hadn't had time to discuss anything. "I thought it might be more fun if we moved someplace new," he said.

Jennie raised her eyebrows at him. "Did you have something in mind?"

"I did." He didn't say anything else. He thought he'd just sit there and tantalize her for a moment. He loved teasing her.

"Are you going to tell us more about this?"

He crossed his arms proudly. "Maybe."

"Michael!"

"Daddy!"

They both hollered in unison and he grinned.

"Well," he said, drawing it out and taking a maddeningly long time. "I've found a place north of town, a small ranch close to Plano. I thought it might be nice to live there."

Jennie looked at him suspiciously, an idea dawning on her. "Have I seen this place by any chance?"

He raised his eyebrows and grinned again. "Maybe."

"Michael!"

Suddenly they were both punching and tickling him. Jennie was saying, "The place where we went riding! Michael, that place is beautiful! Michael!"

"I've—planned—it—for—a—while...." he said, gasping as he tried to fend them off. "I'd given up, though. I figured we weren't ever going to be all together to live there."

He waited until they'd calmed down to tell them that Marge had offered to let them have Bill's horses. "She'll be glad they've got a good home." When he said it, he had tears in his eyes.

"I can't believe this!" Cody kept saying. "I really can't *believe* this!"

"Believe it, son," Michael said, holding him close on the sofa and rumpling his hair. "Believe it. And know that most of it came about because of you. Your bravery has taught your mother and me some important lessons."

Cody grinned from ear to ear as he stuffed popcorn into his mouth. And it was after eleven o'clock before he went to bed. They each kissed him goodnight then they both sat by the fire, holding on to each other as the flaming logs turned into steady embers in the fireplace.

Epilogue

The sun rose over the house in a watercolor wash of color—blues…lavenders…pinks. It would be hours still until the wavering heat of summertime hit the ranch in earnest.

A meadowlark sang out from the dew-covered Johnson grass where once, not so long ago, Jennie and Michael had ridden Dan and Kimbo.

The ranch north of Plano was theirs now. Michael had put the offer in with the Realtor just as soon as Jennie had agreed to marry him. And it had been in Jennie's mind all along that the place would make a lovely backdrop for the wedding.

Upstairs, as the sun moved higher and cast an oblong shape of light on the floor, Cody rolled over and yawned. It was morning. Time to get up. And then he remembered what morning it was! The wedding day! The day his mom and his dad got married all over again.

He flipped back the covers and climbed out, reaching for his chair as his eyes grew even more accustomed to the growing light. Then he rolled across the room to the row of books on the shelf beside his desk. Right beside him, next to the wall, stood the crutches he'd never wanted to use.

Cody pushed his weight forward a bit in his chair and reached for them. They were wonderful things, new and shiny, like swords. As he held them in his lap, he thought about something. Just suppose he should give his mom and dad a wedding present. Just suppose he should try to stand up, right now. Just suppose he should do it. Just suppose.

Slowly, gingerly, he balanced the weight of the crutches in his hands. They felt cool and heavy. Strong. And just right.

He slipped one hand into each one and grabbed on to the handhold. He lowered their tips to the floor. Slowly, slowly, he pushed on them. They held firm. Instead his whole body felt like it wanted to rise up and stand with them. So, he tried it. He clenched his muscles tight just the way Andy had showed him. Then he pushed off.

His arms started shaking like an earthquake. He felt as if he were about to fall and break his head. But he kept at it.

Andy says if I can just do this, I can walk someday, he reminded himself. And, all of a sudden, he had it, he was standing there, straight up like a fence post, and his legs were supporting him.

"Hey!" he said out loud to no one. "Look at me!

Look at this!" That's when he realized he had to show somebody. He started hollering as loud as he could. "Mom! Mom! Mom! *Quick!*"

She came running into his room, still in her night-gown, with her hair all loose and tangled around her shoulders and she looked scared. "Honey? Are you okay?" Then she saw him, and he thought her eyes might pop out of her head. "Cody!"

"I'm doing it!" he shouted at her. "Happy Wedding Day present! I'm doing it!"

"Cody." She ran to him and bundled him up into her arms and he had no idea why she had tears pouring down all over her face. "Oh, Cody!"

"It's your present for today. I'm going to show Dad, too, when he gets here."

"You do that," she said, still crying. "He won't believe it. He'll be just as proud of you as I am."

"I'm standing—I'm standing—I'm standing—" he said over and over and over again.

"You're tall," Jennie said. "I'll bet you've grown three inches at least!" She hugged him. "You did it, Cody," she kept saying. "You did it! You did it!"

"I did!" Cody hollered, throwing his head back and letting it sink in at last. "I did! I did! I did!" He raised one fist and waved it in the air for all of them, a little fist that signaled an enormous victory.

And that was the way the day started.

Someone, one of their many friends who wanted to

make a big celebration out of this wedding, had twisted miles and miles of pink crepe paper along the white corral fences. Someone else had tied a huge satin bow on the front door. Michael and Jennie both wanted the service to be small and simple. But their friends were elated. People brought so much food that the tables were absolutely groaning.

It seemed two o'clock would never arrive. But, by one-fifteen, guests started turning into the driveway. "Hi, Mark!" Cody cried as Mark Kendall climbed out of his car. "Where's Andy?"

"She'll be along in a few minutes. She's coming with Buddy. He stopped by her place to pick her up."

"Buddy?" Cody asked. "Buddy Draper's coming? Wow!"

Marge Josephs came next, carrying a huge bouquet of rosebuds from her garden. They were the exact, delicate color of an eggshell. "These are for Jennie," she said after she'd hugged Michael. "Can I take them up?"

"Sure," he said, giving her one more squeeze. She looked good. Her eyes shone bright and her hair glowed like silver filigree in the sunlight. "They're beautiful."

"They're from Bill's garden." She smiled, a bitter-sweet smile full of love. "He planted them several years ago. They keep coming back."

"How are you feeling?"

She answered honestly. "I'm getting a little better every day. My grandkids are sure keeping me busy."

"Good." He squeezed her forearm. "Grandkids are just what the doctor orders." He glanced up at the window where he knew Jennie waited. "You be sure and tell her those are from Bill."

"I will."

Marge hurried off and the minister drove up. It was time for the service to begin. From just beneath the tree, a college girl they'd hired began to play the *Wedding March* on a lovely old harp. As Michael bid a brief farewell to his friends, he looked around quickly for his best man.

There he was, sitting in his wheelchair beside the harp, dressed in a black tuxedo just his size, exactly the same as his father's. "You ready for this, kiddo?" He winked. "It's time to go stand by the minister."

"I'm ready," Cody said, rolling his wheelchair toward the makeshift altar, his crutches lying across his knees.

"You're sure?" Michael asked.

"I'm sure," Cody answered.

"If you get tired, we'll stop the ceremony and you can sit back down."

They'd planned it all today at lunch, when Cody had presented the wedding present to his father, too. He parked his wheelchair in the appointed spot and, with Michael gripping his elbow, he stood, proud and tall beside his father.

As the harpist strummed softly, out stepped Jennie. Michael had never seen her look more beautiful than she did at that moment, standing in the sun, as she beamed and waved at Cody. She wore a beige satin dress that fell in a straight sheath to the floor, with miniature beige orchids woven into a circlet atop her head. She looked like an angel as she stepped forward, her dress trailing in the lush grass, and came to stand beside them.

"Dearly beloved…" The minister began the vows. Jennie took Michael's hand and squeezed it.

"Love you," she mouthed to both of them.

"Me, too," Michael mouthed back.

When the minister called for the rings, Cody held on to the tree trunk for support and handed his father the ring. "Here you go, Dad," he whispered proudly. "Put this on her."

And, as Michael slipped the wedding ring onto the finger of the woman he loved, the years seemed to sear together in his mind, how he'd wanted Jennie then, how he loved her now.

How much God had blessed them all. How grateful Michael would always be.

He met her eyes and repeated the age-old words, meaning, feeling, every one of them. "For better," which they'd had. "For worse," which they'd had, too.

"In sickness and in health." Perhaps, for now, it would be health. Dr. Phillips had recently confirmed it.

Cody wouldn't need the surgery.

"For richer and for poorer."

"As long as we both shall live," the minister prompted.

Michael gazed down at the woman who stood before him now, at the mother of his son, and he felt as if he'd already loved her forever. Perhaps he had.

He could see the reflection of all he needed in her clear, gray eyes. "As long as we both shall live," he repeated.

QUESTIONS FOR DISCUSSION

1. In chapter one, Michael prays, *Help me to trust You the way my son trusts me.* Even though he asks for this at the beginning of the book, many of his answers don't come until the end. God's response to his prayer is a growing process, not a "quick fix." Describe a life-changing journey in your own life that started when you expected something to happen quickly.

2. Michael feels responsible for Cody's sickness because of his wisdom, because he "ought to have seen something." When Jennie finds out Cody has taken ill, she immediately accuses Michael of negligence. What happened in Jennie's past to cause this reaction? Are there issues in your own past that cause you to cast blame on someone?

3. It is clear that the Heavenly Father had his eye on Cody's healing from the very beginning. Who are the two people God sent into Cody's life to help him overcome his illness?

4. Look up Romans 8:28 and read aloud. How does this scripture apply to Jennie, Michael and Cody? How does it apply to you?

5. When Buddy Draper gives up playing soccer, Andy doesn't understand him because he is a Christian and he's told her plenty of times "Soccer is my calling." Why does Andy walk away from Buddy even though she cares for him? Do you agree with her reasons? Why or why not? In the end, soccer *did* turn out to be Buddy's calling, only in a different form. As Christians, how can we honor the gifts and callings in another person even though we don't understand the direction that person is taking?

6. In chapter seven, Jennie thinks, *I'd give anything for someone to tell me what's right. What's wrong.* Is this the beginning of Jennie's search for God? Why or why not? What does Jennie "let go of" after the Heavenly Father starts nudging at her heart?

7. Have you been in a situation like Andy in chapter twelve when you wanted to talk about the Lord but couldn't because of work or school atmosphere? How did you choose to respond? Are there other ways to share the Lord without speaking up? Explain.

8. Even though Buddy and Andy are not together in chapter thirteen, how does Andy influence Buddy's career and "calling" at this point?

9. When God begins to speak into Jennie's heart, He uses the words from Jeremiah 29:11. Look up this scripture and read it aloud. Why was it so important for Jennie to hear these words at this point? How can these words impact your own life?

10. In chapter sixteen, Michael expresses gratitude to Andy for the ways she influenced Jennie's and Cody's lives. In what ways did Michael have to change to see Andy this way? How would your relationship with God change if you remembered to be grateful for small things in your life instead of taking them for granted? Ask the Heavenly Father to show you these small, daily details. Keep a list and pray over it often.

11. In chapter nineteen, Michael finally admits that the victory has come into his life because he has been willing to "let something go to God" and that, when a person does let go, "sometimes it gets returned to you a thousandfold." What exactly did Michael let go of? What feelings did he let go?

12. What does it mean to really *let something go?* Can you think of something that, when you let it go, God returned to you in a way that you never could have imagined?

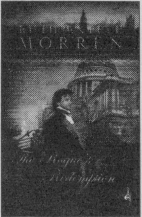

HISTORICAL

INSPIRATIONAL HISTORICAL ROMANCE

Amid the splendors of the Gilded Age, Neala Shaw suddenly found herself entirely alone. The penniless young heiress had no choice but to face her family's fatal legacy of secrets and lies. And as she fled from a ruthless killer, an honorable man unlike any she had ever known stood between her and certain death.

Look for

Legacy of Secrets

by

SARA MITCHELL

Steeple Hill®

Available April wherever books are sold.

www.SteepleHill.com

LIH82785